Praise for Poe

Love & Terror on the Howling Plains of Nowhere

Poe Ballantine is the most soulful, insightful, funny, and altogether luminous "under-known" writer in America. He knocks my socks off, even when I'm barefoot.

TOM ROBBINS, *author of Villa Incognito*

Ballantine's writing is secure insecurity at its best, muscular and minimal, self-deprecating on the one hand, full of the self's soul on the other.

LAUREN SLATER, *author of Lying*

Poe Ballantine is brilliant, sensitive, unique, and universal. Reading his work is inspiring, agitating, and invigorating. He is utterly transparent on the page, a rare thing. He's like a bird that's almost but not quite extinct. This is his best book ever.

CHERYL STRAYED, *author of Wild*

If the delights of either Poe Ballantine or Chadron, Nebraska were a secret, that is over now. *Love & Terror on the Howling Plains of Nowhere* is an unprecedented combination of all of the following: true crime page-turner, violently funny portrait of a tiny Western town, field guide to saving a bilingual marriage and raising an autistic child, sutra on living with open mind and big heart. Many of the sentences start on earth and end somewhere in beat-poet heaven. Ballantine comes ever closer to being my favorite creative nonfiction writer and this is why.

MARION WINIK, NPR *correspondent, author of Above Us Only Sky and The Glen Rock Book of the Dead*

501 Minutes to Christ

Name an author we all need to read? Poe Ballantine's exquisitely funky *501 Minutes to Christ*.

TOM ROBBINS, *Author of Jitterbug Perfume*

Ballantine is never far from the trenches ... the essays are readable and entertaining and contain occasional moments of startling beauty and insight. Still, the themes of addiction (to substances, people, new starts, the prospect of fame), dissatisfaction, and nihilism may limit the work's appeal; as with writers such as Chuck Palahniuk, some will become rabid devotees, while others will be turned off.

LIBRARY JOURNAL

Decline of the Lawrence Welk Empire

It's a downmarket version of Ben Kunkel's *Indecision*, with less surety but real vibrancy.

PUBLISHERS WEEKLY

Ballantine's genial, reckless narrator is part Huck Finn, part Hunter S. Thompson. And in a few pages he's charming you, more than any "pot-smoking, card-playing, music-loving, late night party hound" really should.

THE SEATTLE TIMES

This second novel from Ballantine initially conjures images of *Lord of the Flies*, but then you would have to add about ten years to the protagonists' ages and make them sex-crazed, gold-seeking alcoholics.

LIBRARY JOURNAL

Poe Ballantine, in this sequel to *God Clobbers Us All*, reveals that he is a writer with a keen ear and a blistering wit – it's a prime opportunity to observe a writer's joyful wallow in the decadence of words.

THE AUSTIN CHRONICLE

Edgar's supersize pal Mountain is the best of the author's creations: "He possesses a merry and absurd sweetness ... combined with a body mass that can block out the sun."

BOOKLIST

Ballantine's second novel is ... memorable ... funny and smart.

PHILADELPHIA WEEKLY

Decline of the Lawrence Welk Empire has the same amped tone and subtropical setting as Hunter S. Thompson's *The Rum Diary* but less of the gonzo arrogance and more of that good ol' American angst. The prose is poised on the brink of perfection, and the plot twists into an unexpected yet perfect conclusion that makes scotch and roadkill seem almost palatable.

SAN FRANCISCO BAY GUARDIAN

God Clobbers Us All

It's impossible not to be charmed by the narrator of Poe Ballantine's comic and sparklingly intelligent *God Clobbers Us All*.

PUBLISHERS WEEKLY

Ballantine's novel is an entertaining coming-of-age story.

THE SAN FRANCISCO CHRONICLE

Calmer than Bukowski, less portentous than Kerouac, more hopeful than West, Poe Ballantine may not be sitting at the table of his mentors, but perhaps he deserves his own after all.

THE SAN DIEGO UNION-TRIBUNE

It's a compelling, quirky read.

THE OREGONIAN

Poe Ballantine has created an extremely fast page-turner. Edgar, in first-person narrative, is instantly likeable, and his constant misadventures flow seamlessly. Ballantine paints southern California with voluptuous detail.

WILLAMETTE WEEK

God Clobbers Us All succeed[s] on the strength of its characterization and Ballantine's appreciation for the true-life denizens of the Lemon Acres rest home. The gritty daily details of occupants of a home for the dying have a stark vibrancy that cannot help but grab one's attention, and the off-hours drug, surf, and screw obsessions of its young narrator, Edgar Donahoe, and his coworkers have a genuine sheen that captivates almost as effectively.

THE ABSINTHE LITERARY REVIEW

A wry and ergoty experience.

GOBSHITE QUARTERLY

Things I Like About America

Ballantine never shrinks from taking us along for the drunken, drug-infested ride he braves in most of his travels. The payoff – and there is one – lies in his self-deprecating humor and acerbic social commentary, which he leaves us with before heading further up the dark highway.

THE INDY BOOKSHELF

Part social commentary, part collective biography, this guided tour may not be comfortable, but one thing's for sure: You will be at home.

WILLAMETTE WEEK

Meet the new guide on the lonesome highway. Poe Ballantine's wry voice, clear eye, hilarious accounts and lyrical language bring us up short by reminding us that America has always been about flight, and for most of its citizens it has been about defeat. His wanderings, drifters, bad motels, cheap wine, dead-end jobs and drugs take us home, the home Betty Crocker never lived in. We're on the road again, but this time we know better than to hope for a rumbling V-8 and any answers blowing in the wind. The bus has been a long time coming, but thank God it has arrived with Mr. Ballantine aboard. Sit down, give him a listen and make your own list of *Things I Like About America*.

CHARLES BOWDEN, *author of Blues for Cannibals and Blood Orchid*

Poe Ballantine reminds us that in a country full of identical strip malls and chain restaurants, there's still room for adventure. He finds the humor in situations most would find unbearable and flourishes like a modern-day Kerouac. It's a book to cherish and pass on to friends.

MARK JUDE POIRIER, *author of Unsung Heroes of American Industry and Goats*

Poe Ballantine makes writing really well seem effortless, even as he's telling us how painful writing is. He knows that life is the most funny when it shouldn't be, and that the heart breaks the most during small moments. These stories are shining gems. He kills me, this guy.

MIMI POND, *author of Splitting Hairs: The Bald Truth About Bad Hair Days*

In his search for the real America, Poe Ballantine reminds me of the legendary musk deer, who wanders from valley to valley and hilltop to hilltop searching for the source of the intoxicating musk fragrance that actually comes from him. Along the way, he writes some of the best prose I've ever read.

SY SAFRANSKY, *Publisher, The Sun*

Library of Congress
Cataloging-in-Publication Data

Ballantine, Poe, 1955– author.

Title:
Whirlaway : the great American loony
bin, horseplaying, and record
collecting novel / by Poe Ballantine.

Description:
Portland, Oregon : Hawthorne Books,
[2018]

Identifiers:
LCCN 2017016439
ISBN 9780997068399
ISBN 9780998825700 (ebook)

Classification:
LCC PS3602.A599 W48 2018
DDC 813/.6 – dc23

LC record available at
https://lccn.loc.gov/2017016439

Hawthorne Books
& Literary Arts

9   2201 Northeast 23rd Avenue
8   3rd Floor
7   Portland, Oregon 97212
6   hawthornebooks.com
5   Form :
4   Sibley House
3
2   Printed in China
    Set in Kingfisher

Dedicated to Andy and The Hog,
with special thanks to Marion Winik and Steve Taylor.

LAWAY

POE BALLANTINE

THE GREAT AMERICAN LOONY BIN, HORSE-PLAYING & RECORD-COLLECTING NOVEL

HAWTHORNE BOOKS & LITERARY ARTS
Portland, Oregon | MMXVIII

Contents

WHIRLAWAY

One exists in a universe convincingly real, where the lines are sharply drawn in black and white. It is only later, if at all, that one realizes the lines were never there in the first place.

—LOREN EISELEY

1. Railroaded by Luminescence

AS AN ILLUSTRATION OF WHAT I WAS UP AGAINST AT NAPA STATE Hospital, what they used to call an asylum for the criminally insane, my fellow inmate Arn Boothby, an angry three-hundred-pound paranoid schizophrenic who regularly "cheeked" his meds, tried to kill another inmate one day in the client convenience store by grabbing his throat and throwing him through a glass display case. I was standing in line to buy a pack of breath mints at the time and can attest to him saying, "P.S. I Love You," as the blood spread across the tiles. Boothby was tackled by two psych techs; a staff nurse and hospital police converged within minutes to beat in Boothby's brains behind closed doors. Boothby told me later they would've killed him had not Dr. Fasstink inadvertently intervened. Boothby went to jail, vacation time for most of us at NSH, and I didn't see him at the card game for a few months. When you're surrounded by murderers, bank robbers, arsonists, and child molesters you'll play cards with just about anyone.

And I know what you're thinking (I really do): that I'm innocent, that I don't belong here. Every inmate says this. Well, I'm not innocent, but I should've never been sentenced to a high-security psychiatric hospital full of overmedicated, violent maniacs when I had done nothing but shoplift and make a few crude remarks to women in bars, ride twenty-five-thousand miles on an imaginary bicycle, fancy that I was the ruler of the universe, and run a few delusional undercover operations for the CIA, all brought to you by not taking my meds—or so it was explained to me. I think it was the pattern more than the nature of the violations, and the fact that I had left the halfway house before the expiration of my term, that swayed the judge. Whatever the case, I was mandated by court order to an indefinite term at NSH, and once you're in one of these places you're pretty much at the mercy of the people who run the show.

I did myself no favors at Napa State, for I was outraged to have been placed in a community rife with the worst kinds of con artists, malingerers, and career criminals who'd pled insanity to avoid life sentences in a penitentiary. Then there were the genuinely insane inmates, not a minor case among them, all wandering around freely to do whatever they liked to whomever they pleased. Half the inmate population had killed or tried to kill someone. All the barbers were murderers. One of the barbers, my close friend and first choice for a haircut, Randy Sturtz, had killed his brother and then a neighbor over a cinnamon roll. Cecil Jebb, my roommate for six months, had raped a woman and then tried to strangle her in the parking lot of an Oakland shopping mall, the only time, he liked to brag, that he'd ever been caught. Darvan Laval, a dining companion of mine many evenings who loved to fight, had killed a schoolmate when he was fifteen. Most of the staffers were unarmed women who could not handle the larger, more dangerous male criminals and often had to resort to calling the police. It was no coincidence that about every three months a troublesome inmate would die after a mysterious reaction to an injection or a scuffle with the cops, always behind closed doors.

I was even more outraged at getting thrown into a unit with sexual predators. And since I wasn't, had never been, and would never be a sexual predator, I refused on principle to take the class on sexual harassment, my only official prerequisite besides good behavior for getting released. I also refused the voluntary work. I'd been a journalist in the free world (I had moved from San Diego for a job at the *San Francisco Chronicle*, where I was given the Bay Meadows/Golden Gate beat and my own weekly horseracing column) and I was not about to descend to menial labor in the vulnerable company of barbarous psychopaths. In the first few months I was there a psych tech was murdered by an inmate, the whole hospital went into lockdown. And, though it was always us versus them and this was a good chance for me to be left alone in my room and listen to the radio, many of the staffers took out their fears and frustrations on us, withholding privileges and invoking arbitrary punitive measures, as if we had all conspired to kill their comrade and needed to be taught a lesson. I often felt like that character in the movie *Shock Corridor*, the undercover reporter who commits himself to a mental institution to solve a murder, gets caught up in a riot, receives shock treatment, goes berserk, and never sees the free world again.

At twenty-seven years old I was not emotionally equipped for living under lock and key behind sixteen-foot cyclone fences and having my ass stabbed every three days with drugs that turned my brains to buttermilk. Not only was I bipolar (my original diagnosis, eventually changed to schizophrenia) and prone to dramatic mood swings, I was angry, lazy, selfish, contrary, immature, arrogant, headstrong, and a lover of pranks. I thought I was important because I had invented the now widely used track classification system that distinguishes *primodrome, mezzodrome,* and *llamadrome,* or high, middle, and cheap purse tracks. In case you are not acquainted with horseracing, the system is called the "Plum Variable" or simply "the Plum," as Andrew Beyer's homologous speed figures have simply become "the Beyer." I had also come from a somewhat prestigious family. My father, Calvin Plum, was the notable southern California horse trainer who'd won both the Santa Anita Derby and the Del Mar Futurity twice, and who had also at one time been the largest grower of poinsettias in the world. One of his wives, my third stepmother, had been married to the legendary songwriter Burt Bacharach.

Looking back, it almost seems as if it were my sole mission to never grow up so as to prolong my stay at Napa State indefinitely. Though never a fighter before my commitment, I had to become one to survive, especially when someone tried to play grab-ass with me in the showers (the ones who came at you low you had to get around the neck and the ones who stood their ground you could run into walls with your head and drop them before the attendants came running). I organized the first decent lottery the hospital had seen in years, did not resist the black market (though I stayed away from illegal drugs), participated in numerous tobacco-for-sex arrangements, Vaselined the underwear of my rivals, hosted weekly poker games, invented tranquilizer bingo, and palled up with the killers and fighters so they wouldn't kill or fight me.

In spite of all my shenanigans and refusal to take the harassment class, due to overcrowding, budget and staff cuts, and a long waiting list to get in, the hospital was prepared to release me. The fact that I was one of the few inmates who hadn't committed a felony (I still had the right to vote!) must have nagged the one or two administrators who cared. But then came the incident with Morris, the unit supervisor who was putting the watusi on one of my tobacco girls. He warned me to stop seeing her. I told him in so many words to cram it, so he blew the whistle on me. Half the people in the hospital exchanged tobacco or money for sex, and since we weren't saints but lunatics with needs like all human beings, the hospital usually looked the other way.

But Morris and I didn't get along. I was constantly switching his nametag with those of female attendants (for two hours one day to the giggling of dozens he was "Amy Ocampo. Staff Nurse"), and whenever I could I would glue his pens together. And he needed to deflect attention from his own multifarious misdeeds (including the homebrew he sold black market and the female clients he took home on weekend passes) so he hit me with "sexual aggression," a label that goes a long way against anyone who's already been tagged a sexual predator. Then a mysterious "second party" informed my shrink, Dr. Fasstink, that I was having sex for money with Tasha Little, the thirty-four-year-old mulatto girl on T-17. They had a mini-team on the case and declared that I was "wheeling and dealing." Wheeling and dealing is commendable in free society, but at Napa State it set me back one release hearing at least. Dr. Fasstink, a dainty Latvian with limp wrists and a close-cropped Freudian beard, increased my Haldol from 100 to 125 mg. A few weeks later, Tasha left me for a forty-seven-year-old Cuban fruitcake called Rey Waldo Diaz.

In many cases the staffers, administrators, and psychiatrists were crazier, crueler, and more criminal than the bedlamites they reputedly supervised (note here for the record that Claude Foulk, the director of Napa State, was recently sentenced to 248 years for raping children all the way back to 1965). Napa State was plagued with one sex scandal, drug ring, and unjustifiable death after the next. It was a classic case of the inmates running the asylum, *King of Hearts* without the laughs. And Morris, just to protect his harem and be a hardass and get revenge on me for putting sneezing powder in his Kleenex, placing ads for him in various Bay Area singles' and swingers' papers ("I'm a pink vinyl and diaper-rash ointment kind of guy"), and pouring pancake syrup into his shoes, would bust me for anything—dealing coffee, breaking curfew, playing craps, or changing the channel on the TV without authorization.

Just before my second hearing for release came up, Morris got me kicked off Unit T-15 after I'd told the recreational therapist why I was still at Napa when I could have left long ago. I told her I'd had sex with a hundred female inmates, sometimes two at a time. Her recreational title had misled me and I thought she might be impressed or at least take my elaborate boast in the "recreational" spirit in which it was intended. I certainly didn't think she'd tell Morris, but it turned out *they* were makin' bacon (in his office) and so when he heard the news he told Fasstink and all of a sudden I was a "problem patient," an "operator," and though my various infractions amounted to little more than mischief they somehow through the Constitution of Lunacy qualified me as a "repeat offender" and justified my continued confinement without counsel or trial. For a long time I had my father, the prominent southern California circuit horse trainer, hiring attorneys to get me out, but once he learned that all I had needed from the beginning for a release from Napa State was to take a sexual harassment class he washed his hands of me. The larger point was forgotten, that I had done basically nothing to be sent and kept here indefinitely against my will.

2.   Mudville/
"I Wish It Would Rain"

IT'S DREARY HERE IN MUDVILLE: THE SPIRAL SHADOWS OF THE razor wire against the wire-mesh windows; the hoarfrost rime on the fluorescent bulbs, the milky moonlit halls; the ever-clicking barred and buzzing steel doors and Plexiglas partitioned chambers that make you feel like a poisoned wasp in an electric hive; the yellow-painted rooms and hard little beds; the furtive, whispering, purse-lipped Filipino faces peering at you through parted curtains; the cameras everywhere; the five-point restraints and B52 cocktails—B (50 mg. Benadryl), 5 (mg. Haldol), 2 (mg. Ativan)—when you get out of line; the wailing of inmates and the screaming of the gleaming peafowls; the murders, suicides, beatings, and rapes; the animal rhythm of food, rain, sex, and sleep. And more rain and sleep. And more and more sleep. Mandated biweekly injections of haloperidol (Haldol) blur your vision and destroy your powers. The days and then the years all blend together after a while.

One day they threw a birthday party for me—hamburgers, hot links, potato salad, strawberries, canned jalapenos, watermelon, Diet Dr. Pepper, brownies, and vanilla ice cream. The burgers were fresh ground one-third-pound beef. I ate two and spilled ketchup all over my shirt. It was a gorgeous day, 80 degrees with a slight breeze. Sturtz was there, along with a few other sorry-ass lifers, including Rey Waldo Diaz, Fuckface (no mystery as to how he earned his name), and Boothby with his long nightstick scar like a zipper up the side of his head. Some of the "clients" (as we were called by staff), sore about having been beaten or overmedicated or having had privileges revoked, would not eat the food funded privately for my party (despite the fact that I was an imp I was well liked) by the staff, and instead, in protest ate the crappy state hamburgers. (I was too angry then to thank them for this party. NSH staff, if you're reading this, I apologize and thank you now.) Then they sang "Happy Birthday" to me. I thought it was a mistake when they told me I was thirty-two years old. I even laughed at the thought of totally wasting my life. It was funnier than the ketchup all over my shirt.

But at the party was a new inmate, Sofia Fouquet, twenty-seven years old. I had seen her watching me from a distance. She had a quick way of smiling that I thought at first was cracked or fake but after a time realized was authentic, measured bursts of warmth that seemed solely intended for me. Like me, she had been civilly committed, though she was in for suicide and would not be held long unless she botched her chances as I had. I did not normally get along with women. They were the reason I had been sent to Napa and the reason I stayed here and the reason if I ever get out I will be sent back. They were the torpedo that always sank me. But I could not resist a brooding Mediterranean beauty, cerebral and serene, who wanted to kill herself and who had come to my birthday party. I had also seen one of her photographic exhibitions at a gallery in Ferndale, in Humboldt County, a few years before all my trouble started. Her tide pool and shipwreck photos were as dark and melancholy as she was. She had read my columns and remembered me from her Ferndale exhibition, which she told me was the reason she had come to my birthday party. With a swift, insolent smile she looked at my ketchup stains and asked if I'd been shot.

No such luck, I told her.

We took a long stroll that evening and kept brushing against one another. Haldol is more intoxicating than bourbon, and compounded by the influence of Sofia I could barely walk. Three quarters of the asylum acres were off limits since the psych tech had been murdered, so we kept coming to a fence topped with coiled and glittering concertina wire ("Sure is a lotta barbed wire for a hospital," she remarked at one point), and each time her eyes would blaze and she'd shake her hair and rail at the world outside. Why were we here? By what authority had our inferiors been allowed to put us in this zoo?

I was in full agreement. Our only crime was being born. How we drifted off into the trees I don't remember, but I stumbled and she caught my hand. Sitting Indian style in the flittering shade, our knees touching, we whispered in the language of heat as the green leaves seethed and the words we used ceased to have meaning. Behind the Program 3 office, I kissed her. Too fast, I thought, but she kissed me back and everything shifted underneath and fell away to open space.

It's always easier getting along with someone when you have no future with them, but how nuts is it to meet the woman of your dreams in a nuthouse? To keep creeps like Morris and Cecil from having their way with her, I used my influence and networks to protect her. She called me Big Eddie and said that I was the funniest, bravest person she'd ever met. She spoke a beguilingly fastidious German that convinced many it was genuine until she arrived at the final made-up word in her sentence, *düdüscheiner*, *slutprincessan*, or *das nincompoopen*.

When Morris told me she was undergoing ECT (electroconvulsive therapy), I confronted her.

"It is voluntary," she said. "For depression."

"You must be crazy," I said.

"Shocking, isn't it?"

"You'll lose your memory."

She sucked in her cheeks and crossed her eyes. "Promise?"

In her first month she taped to the wall above her bed a reproduction of Millet's *The Angelus*, which she said Salvador Dalí asserted was not a spiritual or pastoral work as the critics had decided but that the two figures were praying over their buried child. Dalí insisted on this so vehemently, Sofia said, that eventually an X-ray was taken of the canvas, where a painted-over shape similar to a coffin was discovered.

"That is my little baby, too," she said, pointing in the area of the coffin.

"Your baby?"

"Olivia," she said.

"How long ago did you lose Olivia?" I asked.

"It's been five years," she said. "She was only two."

"You are young enough to try again."

She turned away and said, "That is not the point."

Raindrops began to tap the glass then, and I thought of the exquisitely sad Temptations song: "I Wish It Would Rain."

"What is the point?" I asked.

She wiped her face. "It is the same heartbreak every day," she said, fighting tears. "It does not diminish."

"I will try to help you forget," I said. "I have undertaken a Crusade of Oblivion myself. You should quit the ECT and get rid of that morose painting."

"I know." She endeavored a valiant smile. "I cling too fondly to loss." She tore the painting down. "Dalí was an asshole anyway."

Sofia suspended the ECT and joined my Crusade of Oblivion. We gamboled the woods, sneaked off into the back wards, tossed the egg (with the insides blown out so it was hollow) and the coffee can lid. We golfed in the halls, argued about Kafka and grappa, sang improvised camp-fire songs, paid exorbitant underground rates for her precious English cheese, and played gin rummy while sipping from foam cups of smuggled-in cognac before an Amish electric fire.

One day Sofia borrowed a pair of reading glasses, pulled her hair into a bun, and wearing one of Morris's lab jackets went around vis-iting patients and pronouncing in a German accent with her chin nested in her fingers: "Hmmm, well *mein liebchen*, it's obvious you're a cuckoo." We both had level-three ground passes—you could buy one for one or two cigarettes—and we would share courtyard time and go to the commissary and Crossroads together and at every opportunity wander over to T-13 or the S-Complex to use the Gateway computers. I had begun a story about a man unfairly incarcerated in a mental hospital who meets a wandering goddess trapped among the mortals. Once, Dr. Pettipiece, who was widely known to smoke joints with his patients, found us on the monkey bars and hollered at us until he was red in the face. Sofia screeched at the old doper like a chimp and furiously scratched her armpits while I told him in a Ger-man accent that he was obviously a cuckoo.

A hospital is no place to carry on a wine-country romance, so whenever we could we would run off behind the trees. I had not been monogamous since my marriage to my Chinese former wife, Fang-Hua, whom I still loved—though love is neither pain nor betrayal, so I've got the wrong word. The grounds teemed with wild peafowls some eccentric had imported long ago from India in the belief that they would cheer up the residents, even if they shrieked and bred like rats. One time after Sofia and I had made love in the shadows of the woods Sofia began to talk about what we were going to do when we got out and it finally dawned on me what all this meant. The course of my life came to light: I'd run this gauntlet of agony and injustice solely to meet her.

Sofia was out in six months, deceiving her team and meeting all the discharge criteria with flying colors. I kissed her at the gate and looked back at this daft palace of damnation that had held me for more than five years. But my time here was coming to a close. I was young enough to start over, and I knew I could do it with Sofia.

"If I can't get released legitimately," I whispered to her through the bars, "I'll saddle up one of these peacocks and fly out."

"Bring one for me," she whispered back, her sultry brown eyes shimmering. "I always wanted a peacock as a child."

"We'll run away to some foggy little fishing village where you can take gloomy photographs and I'll crank out the great American loony bin novel. And we'll have baby peacocks."

"I love you, Big Eddie," she said. "And I promise to write you every single day."

We held hands until the psych tech dragged me away.

That day I ditched all my schemes, tore up my racket sheets, and took a vow of chastity. I swallowed my Irish pride with two cans of diet root beer and ceased to respond to provocations from patients and staffers alike. I had known all along how to talk to the shrinks but now I saw the wisdom of actually doing it. Like any good conversation, it works best when you show interest in the person you're talking to, so along with agreeing when it was useful, volunteering shopworn phrases such as "becoming proactive," "changing my ways," and "accepting responsibility," guarding their dirty little Bedlam secrets, and massaging regions of credibility that would one day be regarded as fairy tales or mass delusion, I always tried to chat about the doctor's home life—the lawn mower, the daughter at Stanford, and that frustration in the bedroom, whatever they were comfortable discussing. It was not about milking them for information. It was about building trust, making them believe, as Sofia had done, that I was on the mend, that pharmaceuticals and neuroscience and the *Diagnostic and Statistical Manual of Mental Disorders* were the only road to social re-entry for me.

Morris was the hardest to appease. I apologized for all the crap I'd pulled: buying him a muscle magazine subscription, enlisting him in the U.S. Marines, wedging pennies in the jamb of his office door so he couldn't get out, making him look bad on the basketball court, and blowing his cover on the female patients he took home on the weekends. I told Morris he'd have no more problems with me, then bewildered him by giving him all my coffee, cigarettes, and bingo cards. I took over recycling for our unit and within the month we had $147, enough for tri-tip and potato salad instead of the usual nachos and ice cream. I started working fourteen hours a week in the cafeteria, eight in the library, and reluctantly signed up for that sexual harassment class offered twice a year. Whenever Jody, the gay nurse, would give me my Haldol injections he would try and hit my sciatic nerve just to see me jump, but I pretended he was making love to me and moaned with pleasure. I could do anything for Sofia. She stood in the center of my mind like the light of God. I pored over the letters she wrote daily, held them, and smelled them, and taped them to my walls.

Then one day the letters stopped coming. I thought at first that they'd been intercepted, a common practice. The last letter was full of remarks about futility and death and had been signed "Persephone." When I asked that Dinky Russian Stinkpot Dr. Fasstink, he told me with a wiry little smile that Sofia had taken her life. I said in dull shock that I did not believe him. She had jumped from a window, he said, and if I cared to look, the obituary was in the *Chronicle*. I had not been told the news because it would have upset me and possibly required another increase in my antipsychotic regimen, and we didn't want that, did we? The old doctor, wearing an ill-concealed simper, had to help me to the door, saying over and over, "I'm sorry, my lad. I'm sorry, my boy."

3.   Dyskinesia

THE YEARS WHIRLED AWAY LIKE THE VAPOR FROM A BAD DREAM.
But I believe from a comment made by one of the drug nurses after it happened that I was thirty-six when I got into a fight with double-felon Kenny Monique. I probably should not have fought him since he was a habitual criminal who had once boxed professionally, and I had been wandering numbly up and down the corridors, refusing to speak and only eating enough to keep them from feeding me through a tube. But I did not like Kenny, who had murdered a pharmacist and gotten off with an insanity plea, nor did I like being called a "dicklicking Mick." A meth addict with access to Ritalin, he had also learned how to steal diabetic syringes from the treatment room. I had stopped fighting on a regular basis since Sofia had died, so he quickly got the better of me and rammed me headfirst into a wall. Just before I blacked out I thought he had broken my neck and I thought good, but I came to some indeterminable time later with nothing but a black void and buzzing prism-shaped bats across my field of vision, the flesh of my forehead wired together with what felt like guitar string. For a while there was talk of moving me out of circulation, especially since I could see the intermeshing cogs of time and how you could jump between them like a nursery rhyme cow and know for instance the name of the unnerved person who had just entered your room. If I had not regained my eyesight within a few weeks I'm certain I would have gotten discharged from Mudville.

I remember the ceaseless monsoon of winter, and then another wet gray winter, and then Arn Boothby, the three-hundred-pound paranoid schizophrenic who threw a fellow inmate through a glass case, though he really wasn't such a bad guy, died. They said natural causes, but he was only forty-six. He had always told me that after he died he'd come back and tell me what it was like on the other side, so I think it was his spirit that woke me up one day when there was no one else in my room: "None of this is as bad as you think," the voice whispered, "and God is a chocolate donut." It was Boothby's laugh, without a doubt, and I laughed too, the first time a sound like that had passed from my lips since Kenny Monique had bulldozed me into that wall.

Since random sex takes about fifteen minutes and the three meals all told take about an hour and a half and the horned peacock in the oak tree outside your window makes sure you only get eight hours of sleep a night, there is a lot of unfilled time and by the time I turned forty I'd borrowed and read every book at NSH, and had become something of an expert on trivial subjects, especially pop music. I'll tell you, sitting there in your living room, it's a lucky thing we've got these snake pits like Napa so that we can keep people like Sturtz, the barber who killed his brother over a cinnamon roll, out of the general population. But the guy was bright, and for hours in his room we'd play "What's that tune?"—a cigarette for every song you guessed right first. I'd usually come out after thirty or forty songs, six or seven cigarettes ahead. Cigarettes went for ten dollars or more apiece, so for a single smoke you could get a bottle of Morris's homebrew, a high-level ground pass, an extra hour of television, or the butter-roasted whole walnuts or halvah that Zaahida in T-6 received from her Uncle Baba in Jordan.

Sturtz, whose family had lived in Napa Valley for over a century, told me that Napa State had once been self-sufficient, a sylvan, sprawling, magnificent Vermont-slate, Florentine-Moorish castle with its own gardens, orchards, bakery, dairy, livestock, carriage houses, barns, forges, newspaper, and cemetery. Originally constructed as a spillover for Stockton Asylum, Napa Asylum for the Insane, since it was located deep in the hinterland, took Stockton's worst cases, the "chronically insane." Staff and patients lived together on the same grounds. Like monks, they made whatever they needed: shoes, clothes, music, cheese, coal gas, furniture, bread, even beer. An underground railroad conveyed meals and laundry to the various wards. Patients were rarely discharged, they simply finished their lives here. Among these were paupers, the homeless, those without family, the invisible class. As the years passed and the city and lucrative wineries and vineyards closed in around the asylum, monastic self-sufficiency gradually gave way to urban interdependency and the techno-electro-chemical revolution. It was the Age of Anxiety and the Benighted Soul. With Mudville's eventual designation as "forensic" (criminal), sixteen-foot razor-wire-crowned fences were installed.

In the days of its idyllic independence, thousands of patients had been buried at NSH, though most of the markers had been uprooted and displaced over time. Sturtz thought that some of the bodies of those who died questionably or unjustly must have been hidden in Mudville walls, for occasionally the corridors reeked with the odor of death. Countless efforts to unearth the source, basement and attic explorations, left the matter unexplained. Perhaps it was the many catastrophic river and sewer floods that had swamped the town and its storied madhouse and subway tunnels, or possibly, I suggested, it was some ghastly immaterial remnant of those who had departed unhappily from these premises.

"Yeah, but who sang 'Build Me Up Buttercup?'"

"The Foundations. And don't call me Buttercup."

"Bingo, Daddy-O."

You're always told when you're going to get out, four months, seven months, two years, six if you're a good little boy or girl, and you'll tell everyone as if you just won a ticket to Wonka's chocolate factory: "I'm getting out in *four months.*" It is the highlight of any inmate's life (and for most of us a chance to unleash once again on society). I had been told many times that I was going to get out, but something always came up, and it was plain after a while that my fate was stamped, that I was going to stay here forever with the killers and the cuckoos and the cons.

Death is one of God's better ideas, and I was ready to jump into its sweet marshmallow middle with the faint hope that I would somehow find Sofia Fouquet on the other side. But then one day after one of the aides reminded me that another year had passed and it was now my forty-first birthday this ruddy, broad-chested, clear-eyed man with a nose like a boat rudder and a forehead upon which you could've set a dinner for four, and these long soft plumes of gray hair down to his shoulders, strolled into my room, hands in the pockets of his smock. I was listening to the radio, having a Diet Pepsi, and staring at my misogynist Hoopa roommate, Earl Nez, who never talked but always shared with me his acorn bread. The shrinks were all alike, so I didn't waste much energy on them. He introduced himself as Dr. Horace Jangler and said he had taken over for Fasstink.

"Terrific," I said. "I hope he fell off a bridge."

Jangler said that Fasstink had retired.

I said that did not preclude him from falling off a bridge.

"Oh, an optimist," he said with a chuckle and asked if I'd like to take a walk.

I hadn't been outside in memory, and the sun hurt my eyes. We followed the trails that reminded me of Sofia. Dr. Jangler unlocked a gate and we hiked down into a heavily wooded area where the inmate population was normally not allowed. At the bottom of the trail was a lake upon which floated a single black swan. Dr. Jangler gestured to a stone bench under an ash tree and asked me to sit. I declined his offer of a cigarette. "I don't smoke money," I said.

"Nor should you," he replied. "Nasty habit."

"Pretty lake," I said. "Never been down here."

"Do you miss San Diego?" he asked.

"Doubt if I'd recognize it."

"It's the same city," he said, "just bigger, that's all." He mentioned a few San Diego institutions, the Chart House, Saska's, Mister A's, the lowly Padres, the Belly Up Tavern, all still in operation.

"What about Golden Hall?" I said.

"Still there."

"I saw Neil Young there."

"I saw the Grateful Dead there."

I said that I had seen the Grateful Dead at Golden Hall too.

"Imagine that," he said with a grin. "We might've even been sitting next to each other."

"I would've been too drunk to notice."

"That open bar," he said, with a fond wag of the head. "I see your father is Calvin Plum."

"The Great Calvin Plum," I replied, unable to muster any enthusiasm.

"I know all about your Plum Variable. Used to use it myself. Once, long back when I was teaching at Tulane, I got six winners at Louisiana Downs strictly using Plum and closing quarter fractions."

"No charge," I said.

"They've got you in the SDSU Hall of Fame."

"No, really?"

"I'm an Aztec, too." He puffed up a bit. "Graduated '81."

"The year before me," I said.

"Funny we never ran into each other."

"Big campus," I said. "And I never took any psych classes. Probably should have. Ha."

He watched my right foot shaking up and down and side to side.

"Dyskinesia," I said. "From the Haldol."

He wiped his hand down his face and stared down at the water. "This is my first hospital job," he explained. "Had no idea what was going on here. Appalling conditions."

"Chamber of Horrors," I said.

He rubbed his chin. "First thing I did was review the histories of all my patients who hadn't committed felonies. Pretty short list." He paused. "You don't belong here."

"I've been telling them that since I arrived."

He lit himself another cigarette. "When was the last time you were outside?"

"Had my appendix pulled a few years ago."

"Why don't we take a drive through the country tomorrow?"

4.   Life Begins at Forty-One

EVERY AFTERNOON FOR THE NEXT FOUR DAYS I'D CLIMB INTO DR. Jangler's black BMW with Boston or Beethoven playing and we'd drive out the hospital gates and into the valley, following the river and the contours of the green hills with their overgrown chateaus and rows upon rows of world-class grapes. Jangler would smoke, periodically tapping his cigarette into a little bean-bag ashtray on the dash. He rarely talked about matters psychiatric; instead it was mutual San Diego-flavored ground, old girlfriends or Dave Winfield or the great nine-year-old-thoroughbred John Henry, the Charity Ball, or the bare breasts of Miss Emerson at the Over-the-Line Tournament. Each day we stopped at the same Italian restaurant, where he encouraged me because I was so thin to go for the butter and cream. I knew he was studying me to see how I might behave in the free world. I always put my napkin in my lap and chewed slowly with my mouth closed.

At the end of the week we met in his office. He had his feet on the desk. "There's only so much I can do here, Eddie," he said, hands folded on his chest. "I've replaced an old regime, but the new one I'm afraid isn't much better. There's a lot of public pressure on this institution to keep its inmates out of the community." He paused. "But I think if you can agree to a few things, taking that class, of course, and doing some volunteer work with a few of the patients, there's a good chance I can get you out of this."

"I can't take that class," I said. "I signed up before, but that was to see Sofia. And now she's gone. If I took that class now it would be admitting I'm a sexual offender, and I'm not. What else have I got left but my integrity? I said a few lousy things to some women I didn't know, but

I never touched any of them. I'm not a violent person, except in this cesspool of maniacs where I'm forced to defend myself."

"I applaud your stand," he said. "But you'll have to meet me halfway on this, otherwise I won't be able to help you. If you don't learn to compromise you'll never get out of here."

"All right. And the haloperidol?"

"I've cut your dose in half. We'll see how you do."

That Sunday I went to church for the first time in twenty years, attending the Protestant service because it was shorter and I liked the pastor, a Japanese antilapsarian dentist named Watanabe. Once again, I signed up to take the harassment class and re-enrolled for volunteer labor in the laundry and canteen. I also started attending AA meetings and began to work with some of the schizophrenics in my unit on T-12, one in particular, a crippled twenty-eight-year-old named Jericho Sunday. A high school football star from the East Bay, Jericho had tried to kill himself by driving his '95 Camaro off a cliff. At great speed, before he could make the cliff's edge, he smashed into a tree, permanently damaging both legs. Because he walked in a stiff-legged fashion like an emu or an elephant bird and had not been able to get airborne on his suicide flight before hitting that tree, everyone called him Flightless.

Flightless had angels in his head. He'd say, "My angels tell me you're a dirty butthole," or "My angels won't let me buy commissary today." And if his angels told him something, that was it. But his angels were also telling him to punch staff members in the face and he would get up during TV shows and fight with female employees. The guy was six-four, 265, about my size before I quit eating. They called him The Enforcer when he played linebacker in high school.

So he was put on one-to-one, round-the-clock supervision by at least one staff member. I got him off one-to-one by telling him jokes, buying him cans of pop, and talking about horses and football and his favorite team, the Cal Golden Bears. The breakthrough came when he lent me his *Sports Illustrated* and we laughed about Dusty Baker yanking Russ Ortiz in the seventh so the Giants could swirl down the toilet. "Champagne on ice and so is Disney," he said, which is the way the voices used to sound in my head, too, until the Haldol and the lithium carbonate made them go away. Anyway, I gave Flightless back his *Sports Illustrated* within twenty-four hours, won his trust, and eventually he was assigned one-to-eight staff coverage and could sleep with his door closed instead of having to have his door propped open and a staffer sitting with him in his room.

I also worked with a kid who had shot three people at his high school and a serial rapist (they always seem to have prostitutes for mothers) and a Taiwanese pedophile named Vic Wang, and since I was more sympathetic to their situations, understood personally their stunted development, disgraceful upbringing, festering minds, was not afraid of them, and refused to use words that contained the root *psyche*, I think I was more effective in many cases than the shrinks or the techs themselves.

After I'd taken the harassment class and passed the exam, Dr. Jangler took me for a long drive. He was strangely quiet. It was a Friday. He went to the river just past downtown Napa and parked along the wall. We got out. He stared at the river. "Got some bad news and some good news," he said.

I nodded.

"Bad news is I can't get you out."

"Why not?"

"You've built up too much rancor. You've got this ticky-tack rap sheet a mile long. Most of them up there would just as soon see you rot at Napa State."

"What's the good news?"

"Good news is you don't have to go back if you don't want to."

"What do you mean?"

"I'm busting you out."

"How?"

"I'll just tell them you bolted and jumped into the river. I followed but lost you. It's stated explicitly in your record that you don't know how to swim. In my opinion you drowned. Frankly, I think that will come as welcome news. I'm driving back to San Diego tonight. You can ride with me while they drag the marsh. You've got people there, yes?"

"It's been a long time since I've been back, but a few, yeah, and my father."

"Don't look so flabbergasted, Eddie."

"But how can you do this?"

"How can I not do this. You've spent more than a third of your life in a mental hospital because you stole some *suits*?"

"Aren't you going to get into trouble?"

"Patients escape all the time. Anyway, I'm not sticking around much longer myself."

"Where are you going?"

"Don't know yet. Who knows? This place is a discredit to the human race. I've never seen such deplorable treatment of patients. I had no idea what I was getting into when I accepted this position." He drew a package of cigs from his smock pocket, shook out and lit one. "Besides, I'm not really a psychiatrist."

"What?"

"I was a theater major at San Diego State."

"How did you…"

"I'm an actor, and a pretty fair one at that, but it's hard to get steady work. So I create my own roles. In the last decade I've been a trial lawyer, the mayor of Reno, and the captain of an oil tanker. Before that I was a literature professor at Tulane. Certain jobs are all about presentation. I'm thinking about becoming a cosmologist next, all you have to say is 'quantum vacuum field' and the audience is yours. Anyway, if you're up for it I've brought you a change of clothes and a little disguise." He opened his trunk. "Get into all this after I've gone. I'll pick you up in front of that Italian restaurant around six, how does that sound?"

"What about my medications?"

"I can write you all the scrips you like, but my suspicion is that you don't need them."

"But you're not a psychiatrist."

"We'll iron out the fine points later. Right now I need to get back and report you missing. So plunge down the bank and dash along the river there, if you don't mind. I'll shout at you a few times from the window, and then I'll see you in about three hours. You remember where the Italian restaurant is?"

5. Chivalrous Deceptions

I SLEPT MOST OF THE LONG DRIVE SOUTH. THE WARM, GLOWING green chamber of Jangler's BMW was like a return to the womb. Freedom was out there in the night with the city lights like unfriendly faces. I recalled the prostitute at the Mustang Ranch outside of Reno who had explained to me with a sneer just before I fell apart how I was one of the favored millions who lived on the degradation of the rest. My dreams were vivid and bizarre. In one I was going to bet a horse I felt good about. A tiny Chinese man had his twisted head sticking out of a wall, behind which I found a basement room, inside of which was a very cool couple in their fifties, a man with white hair pulled back into a ponytail and his attractive and buxom black wife. The room was furnished in an early capital-punishment theme and filled with endearing frippery such as whirling monkeys on bronze seats, an empty radioactive canister, some sharpened battle axes, and a television that was covered until a second glance revealed it was not covered. I had had many psychic episodes and prophetic dreams, and they had all spelled disaster, yet hope remained that this was my future, that the ethereal man in the dream was me.

The rising sun was lighting the ocean when Jangler took the Via De La Valle exit off of Interstate 5, turned down the ramp and pulled into the Denny's parking lot just around the corner from the Del Mar Racetrack. It is cool here every morning, the tentacle shrouds and mists crawling in off the sea. Denny's had always been a joke, with papery, undercooked hash browns, greasy, slippery eggs, and overcooked spaghetti, but this morning it felt like a godsend. We took a booth by a window.

The waitress appeared, her nametag read: SHEILA.

"Coffee?" I asked.

Sheila was confused. "Yes," she said. "We…have coffee."

"I haven't had a cup in years. Coffee is black market where I come from."

Now Sheila looked worried.

Jangler laughed. "He's been in a quantum vacuum field."

"Oh," she said.

I stared at the menu. My hands were shaking (the tremor is still with me). Jangler ordered for us. The coffee came. Coffee was black market at Napa because it was considered a drug. Two gulps in and you could appreciate why. I began to hum. I poured in some cream. The sun cracked a cloud and lit the room.

We ate with the sun drenching the orange freckles on the backs of my trembling hands. Jangler looked tired but serene. I saw him pulling chivalrous deceptions wherever he went as he amused himself in the pursuit of a higher cause. No one had ever taken this much risk on my behalf (it felt almost *fatherly*) and it made me intent on success, however that might be defined, outside asylum walls.

After we'd finished eating he slid across an envelope. Inside was loose cash and the driver's license of a shellac-faced and felonious looking longhair named Willie Wihooley. "They had a bunch of drivers' licenses left over from dead patients," Jangler explained, "and I picked the one that looked most like you. Irish at least. It's expired, but you can get it renewed. The DMV doesn't do background checks. You see there are some scrips in there, for Haldol, clozapine, some tricyclics, tranqs, whatever you think you might need. Write to me or call if you need more, codename Willie. Probably best to have them filled in Mexico."

"Where did the money come from?"

"Discretionary funds. Thirteen hundred was as much as I could raise. I threw in a bit of my own. Call it a donation to a good cause."

"Long as you don't try to claim it as a deduction."

"The state owes you a lot more than that. They owe you a new life."

"I don't care. I'm just glad to be free."

"If you want to stay free you'll take my advice. Pursue a modest and contemplative existence. Be honest with yourself. Above all, avoid stressful and potentially dangerous situations, especially anything to do with women."

"That's a tall order."

He sipped from his juice. "You don't need to be Carl Jung to figure out the cause of your trouble. Your mother left you when you were seven."

"And I never saw her again."

"And your wife Fang-Hua left you when you were in your midtwenties."

"I didn't think a Chinese girl would dump me. Quite the blow to my ego when she did."

"That was when your descent began."

"The 'psychotic trigger,' as Fasstink calls it."

"You're aware of the pattern?" he asked.

"Women problems."

He nodded vigorously. "You're unable to trust and therefore to love. Been divorced twice myself, so I can relate. Point is, if you realize that all your sorrow stems from women, just stay away from them. And until you're back on your feet, avoid all sensory overload situations—fights, bars, football games, walking through graveyards at night. You know San Diego. There are plenty of low-stress arrangements. Get a job as a gardener and a little room downtown. I wish I could do more for you, but freedom is something you have to earn on your own. That's what makes it precious."

Jangler had to get running. An oil change at Jiffy Lube and then a fishing trip at Lake Miramar with his eldest son. He asked if I needed a ride anywhere. I replied that I might just stretch my legs and get some air. My father's house in Solana Beach, I told him, was not far away.

Outside, we shook hands. I tried to thank him but he waved me off. "You'd've done the same for me. Godspeed, Eddie. And if you need anything, don't hesitate to call or write. Again, just use the name Willie."

He stared at me for a few seconds, then bowed his head, turned on his heel, and strode away. I listened to his black BMW purr as it left the lot, moved through the green light, and curved gently away up into the pillared dusty benzene thunder of the interstate.

6.   The Key's in the Ashtray

SANTA ANITA WAS RUNNING THIS TIME OF YEAR, SO MY FATHER would not be in his Solana Beach house but in his condo in L.A. I would've called him but I didn't remember his number. Hands in pockets, I strolled over to the track. There was a guard at the main stable gate I didn't feel like talking to, so I walked down Jimmy Durante Boulevard and then across the long parking lot. There was some kind of antique car show going on. A good-sized satellite facility had opened on the fairgrounds since I'd been here last.

The track was much larger than I remembered with lots of new towers and decks. I waved at the tile mosaic of Don Diego and got a drink of water at the fountain, then I found my way backside, walked past the training track, through maintenance, down the empty shedrows. I said good morning to two dark, short muckers wearing white cowboy hats and white rubber boots up to their knees, the only souls to be found. Most everyone else was on the circuit and would not return to Del Mar until July. At the racing office I asked for my father's phone number.

"Who are you?" the secretary wanted to know.

"I'm his son, Eddie Plum."

"I didn't know Cal had a son."

I was shaky and pale and my face was slumped. I was tenuous and perspiring and not making a good impression. "We're not that close."

She opened a book. "You want the one in Culver City, Arcadia, or Solana Beach?"

"Arcadia."

She scribbled on the back of an envelope and slid it across. "You do look kind of like him."

I dialed the number at the payphone outside the stable café, which was closed. I had good memories of this place from my childhood, the long tables, the bare wooden floor, all the hard, short men in riding boots and helmets eating crackers and soup and toast without butter so they could make weight, the smell of manure and frying bacon and damp hay, the columns of dusty sunshine piercing the windows and the rat-a-tat-tat of Spanish in the air.

My father sounded annoyed when he answered. I felt lucky to catch him. I'd never gotten along with him. He was a child of the Depression and the son of a strict Ohio Calvinist minister, a workaholic who was troubled that my generation was not as respectful or strong or hardworking as his. Growing up, I would not see him for weeks at a time. He worked sixteen-hour days, taking only Christmas off. He'd been married five times. His first wife, my mother, had left when I was seven and I barely remembered her. I never liked any of his other wives, and I don't think any of them liked me. He had taught me a lot about horses, hoping I would join him on the backstretch one day, but I preferred the front side, the gambling element, the frivolous, lazy, parasitic element, as my father regarded it. Journalism was another pursuit he didn't support. There were the people who did things, he liked to say, and the people who talked about them, the second group having, in his opinion, no value. More and more people every day paid to do nothing but talk, he liked to say. When Fang-Hua left me and my life fell apart, I was only reaping in his view what I had sown. Though he had hired me several lawyers, he had come to visit me on only three occasions the whole time I was at Napa, all three brief side trips from his primary business at Bay Meadows or Golden Gate Fields.

"Dad," I said. "This is Eddie."

"Yeah, Eddie," he said.

"Well, I'm out," I said.

"That's what I heard. They called me last night. What do you think you're doing anyway?"

I felt boyish when I replied, "They had no right to keep me."

"So, what are you going to do now? They catch you they'll throw away the key."

"They'd already thrown away the key. Have you got a place I can stay?"

A long pause followed before he said, "Should be a couple of cabins at the Island. Go talk to Beatriz. Do you remember Beatriz?"

I said that I did.

"They're all fugitives up there, so you should be safe."

"Do you have a vehicle I can use?"

"Sure, there's an old truck in Del Mar backside, parked in a shed. We use it to haul hay. The key's in the ashtray. Good luck finding someone to let you in."

"Thanks, hey, I know you're busy, so I'll catch you down the way, we'll have dinner or something."

"If anyone asks, I never heard from you."

That was about as close to kind words as I could ever expect from my father.

7.   Island of the Butterscotch Beast

A ROUND, BANDY-LEGGED LITTLE FELLOW WEARING A PONCHO and a wide tooled belt with a silver buckle on it as big as my fist rolled up to me as I wandered around the backstretch looking for the shed where the truck might be parked. The entire area, like the main track facility itself, had been reconfigured and I had no idea where my father's stables might be. I asked him in Spanish if he knew Calvin Plum. He pointed to a row of stalls, one containing a horse, the name plate on the bridle of which read "Bug Eyed Joe." I explained that I was going to get the truck and asked him which of the sheds he thought it might be in. The key, I told him, as if this were some special password, was in the ashtray. He shrugged as if I'd told him I had decided to breathe now. All the shed doors were unlocked and on the third door lifted I found the truck.

The clutch was longer than I thought it should be, but other than that driving returned naturally to me. The guard at the gate gave me a funny look as I rolled past him probably thinking that I was a member of the antique car show who'd gotten turned around. I went up the boulevard slowly, my eyes sweeping from mirror to mirror and fixing repeatedly on the crack in the windshield. It was early enough in the morning and late enough in the season that there wasn't much traffic. I drove under the interstate bridge and headed inland up into the bluffs to the Island, as my father called it, or *Isla Escondida* (Hidden Island), as most of the Latinos who resided there preferred.

Back in the 1950s my father had bought this isolated parcel of land for a few thousand dollars (it had to be worth millions now) and put up a few *casitas* for his hired help, 99 percent of whom were Mexican. My father was a great admirer of Mexicans, principally for the small wages and low maintenance they required. He also had some flower greenhouses built for my mother. Horticulture was all the rage in the sparsely populated north county then. He bought extravagant gifts for all of his wives, trying to make up for never being home. When my mother left him the poinsettia houses went untended. I had many memories of running through their hot feral and earthy halls, lying sedate in the filtered green sunlight when it was cold outside. Very young, I'd been warned that the poinsettia was poisonous, and since then I'd mysteriously associated the scarlet Christmas flower with Babar the Elephant and the death of his mother.

From the road below, you would not have known that this little outpost existed. It had perhaps been Spanish missionaries who'd planted a windbreak of oaks on the west side that through their tangled branches on a clear day you could see the spangled blue-gray prairie of the Pacific Ocean. On the eastern side was high bluff. To the north were the empty hothouses, beyond that the Spanish colonial ceramic-roofed and beige stucco monotony that constituted the new architecturally conformist southern California as far as the eye could see. The southern end was open but occluded by citrus, avocado, and eucalyptus trees. I drove up the narrow, crude road and parked next to a brown Cozy Craft van with four flat tires. As the giant oaks swayed, their leaves made a fizzing sound in the breeze.

I found Beatriz in her garden behind *casita* number 1. She did not recognize me until I spoke. Beatriz had a round face and slanted eyes like an Eskimo. I remembered her as young, but now like me she was not so young. She smiled at me and touched my waist with her wrist. In her company was a big dog, half St. Bernard, half pit bull, a giant barrel-chested, stumpy-legged orange and white lummox who looked like something out of Tolkien or *Where the Wild Things Are*. His name was Carlito and it was plain that he did not like me. He growled and lowered his head and showed his teeth. Beatriz smacked him on the head and said, "*Ya ni la haces, pulgiento.*" He continued to growl at me, so she pointed and said, "*Vete, cabron, desgraciado*" until he slunk away, cowing but still looking back to glower at me, his muzzle flickering with hatred. I knew that he'd kill me given the chance and I formulated a plan to brain him with a fireplace poker the next time I saw him.

Beatriz only shook her head as I explained my situation. I

blurred but did not directly lie about my reasons for being here, explaining that my psychiatrist had released me against the will of the administrators and that my father had given his blessings on a cabin for a few months. All of this seemed a painful subject for her, and I knew that due to lack of food and attention I did not look well, so I asked her about her six children. They were all gone, she said sadly, scattered across the country. The closest was her daughter in Temple City. There was a son in the siding business in Mendocino, another a policeman in San Antonio, a daughter in Gilroy who was a real estate agent. She didn't see them as much as she liked. I asked her why she stayed here and she said she did not know, but I thought out of loyalty to my father and as a maternal influence over the *migrantes* who flowed through here in their various labor circuits.

"*Apareces muy cansado*," she said, and I said that, yes, I was quite tired. She smiled thinly and touched me again at the waist with her wrist, then went inside to get me the key to number 7.

While I waited for her return I strolled the grounds. This miniature barrio was composed of seven *casitas* arranged in a circle around a central orange tree that had doubled its size since I'd seen it last. The tree was loaded with sparrows and fruit and the sharp citrus aroma sent me back. Each small bungalow was identical, with a small deck and the long troughlike metal barbeque pit they called a *parilla* in front of it. All the residential units were stained brown, the color of cabins in the woods, but each was decorated differently: one had a hammock, another a basketball hoop, several had hanging pots or porch swings or saints in the windows or flower boxes or glittering broad ceramic planters with geraniums. Two of the *casitas* had *Familia Catolica* plaques above the door. Another had a *Chivas El Mejor Equipo Del Mundo* sticker in the window. They were all uninhabited except for Beatriz's and mine.

My cabin was furnished in the style of the 1970s, cracked vinyl sofa with matching wing chair, swanky tasseled ottoman, round-shouldered refrigerator with a handle like a slot machine, braided hippie rugs, and an ancient plaid dinette set. The wallpaper was yellow with rainbows. An old JCPenney stereo record player stood in the corner with a row of Tito Puente and Celia Cruz albums in the cabinet below. In the kitchen was an old black rotary telephone that weighed four pounds and still worked. There were a few paintings on the walls, a tarnished oceanscape, a woodland scene with deer looking up startled from a stream, an amateur's crude blue velvet portrait of a high-collared Elvis. In the kitchen cupboards I found a bottle of malt vinegar, a cellophane bag of *japones* chiles, a half-wrapped chunk of *Abuelita* chocolate, a bottle of crystallized fish sauce, a jar of *cajeta*, some stale sesame crackers, a blue box of Don Pedrito herbal remedy, and an unopened can of cashews. In the fridge was a crusty bottle of *Valentina*, a package of old tortillas, a pair of wrinkled limes, half a bottle of white wine, and a cheesecloth-enveloped ball of *queso fresco*. I recognized it as the kind that Beatriz made, too salty and tasting slightly of unwashed feet, but good with beans or sprinkled like parmesan on noodles. I was happy to find not only a coffeemaker but a big blue can of Maxwell House coffee beside it.

The mattress on the bed was queen-sized, wide as a battleship, and the sheets though dusty were fresh with the scent of marshmallows and wound all around me like kelp around the ankles of a man washed up exhausted on a deserted shore. I slept for three days, maybe it was four. Beatriz brought meals, that lentil dish with the dried corn that I liked and stacks of warm tortillas that I ate with the *queso fresco*. I could hear the ocean far off and the occasional pounding of hooves. Carlito, that colossal butterscotch splotch of a malevolent beast, stood under the orange tree and scowled at me through the window.

8. Dr. Seuss in the Sky

WHEN MY LAST HALDOL INJECTION WORE OFF I DECIDED NOT TO take anymore. What is the purpose of liberty if you are chained to a chemistry set and jerking around spastically like a marionette on the strings of an evil puppeteer? Just say no to drugs: *echale ganas*. If I started spitting and raving or thinking I was Napoleon I could always fill one of Jangler's scrips. There were dozens of pharmacies in the north county, one on every corner and one in every grocery store.

Nervous was I like Dr. Seuss in the sky, and then I'd drink coffee and really fly, but my mind had not been allowed to work freely in ages, and I saw once again the infinite transcendental landscape of the mind and how everything, even death, was aperiodically interactive in quasicrystalline symmetry and I lay on the hardwood floor or on that cracked black couch and watched the electric storms behind my eyelids and wondered maniacally about time and why if the eardrum is simply a single vibrating membrane like a tiny trampoline how it can discern every detail of every instrument in a symphony orchestra along with the old man coughing next to you.

As the drugs began to evaporate from my system the simple beauty of my surroundings unfolded: I savored the fresh air and the clouds and the sand under my bare feet, the cool-aired supermarkets with their acres of delicacies, the crackle of a freshly opened *Racing Form*, and no one looking over my shoulder or following me down a corridor with a syringe in their left hand. Never again would I take for granted a private bathroom, the choice to drive east or west without permission, or a long walk down to the beach at night to watch the caps and veins of foam in the curling faces of the moon-painted waves. Like a child, I was once again in awe of flowing water, disheveled movie theaters, sitting around the house naked with a freshly opened tub of Cool Whip, and never once answering the phone.

After two weeks off my meds I also began to get my telepathic powers back. Beatriz was often away, leaving no one to watch Carlito, so he hung around scowling and growling at my door, waiting for his opportunity to maul me, and I would've gotten him first if I'd had a fireplace poker, but as the heavy haze of boundless years of pernicious and addictive medicines lifted I realized that he was not the threat I had originally perceived.

To make amends, I invited him in. He wagged his tail and said to me in so many words, *if you give me even as much as an old tortilla I will stay here and help to heal your mind.*

How did you know I had tortillas? I asked him.

It is written all over you, he replied.

Your name is not really Carlito, is it?

No, I am not a Mexican dog.

You look like a big butterscotch sundae.

Flattery will get you nowhere.

From now on I will call you Sweets.

You are about the most pathetic human being I have ever seen.

That made me laugh for what Sweets said was true.

All I had were curly old dried-up tortillas, which Sweets preferred for their chewy staleness, but I didn't have enough for his liking so I gave him some of the *queso fresco,* which he snuffled at because he said it gave him the runs. I fell asleep at noon in a patch of sun on the floor and woke up with the front door wide open and that big snoring orange-and-white brute piled into my ribs and I knew that he had begun to heal me. Later that afternoon, I took him swimming in the ocean, and on the way back I picked up a thirty-pack of Mission tortillas from Vons and set them out on the kitchen table to dry.

Freedom presented problems that I hadn't had to worry much about in Mudville, chief among them money and sex. Without rent and not much interest in eating, I'd be all right financially for a while. Eventually I'd have to get a job or develop a gambling system or write a bestseller or something to that effect, but off the noxious psychotropics my libido was sharp to the point of an overload if not addressed. I knew no eligible women and did not want to compromise my situation or troll lucklessly in a bar, so I drove down to Tijuana, which had been transformed into a modern city since I'd seen it last. All my old haunts were gone. The Jai Alai Palace had closed. Agua Caliente, the preeminently fast and crooked lla-madrome (cheap-purse track) that only ran on the weekends, had burned down twice before they'd finally closed it for good (horse tracks burn down at disproportionate rates, almost always by a vengeful hand). Most of the clubs and restaurants I'd frequented had assumed new names and facades.

I had never liked *La Zona Norte*, where the tourists and the drunken college kids rented their overpriced and diseased prostitutes, but my favorite whorehouse on *Espejo* had moved, and the Chicken Brothel on *Avenida Revuelto* was now a language school. I drove my truck until I couldn't smell the river anymore, parked on a side street, and wandered into a bar where all the *paisanos* looked up at me as I came through the door as if I were an ostrich. Indeed, in the mirror I did look like an ostrich. I had a shot and a beer and listened to the *cumbia* on the jukebox. Some *vaquero* threw a firecracker under my chair which got me so rattled I almost laid him out as everyone in the confounded place laughed, but here I recognized was a *test*, which I decided to *pass* since if I were arrested in Mexico it might be my last act in the free world, and anyway I had come for love not war.

It is always best to go off the main track looking for whores. They are floozier on the fringes, cheaper, sweeter, more discreet. So I wandered down the street until I came to a little wooden two-story Moroccan looking hotel with dahlias and marigolds in big broken-mirror pots on the wrought iron balconies and six brightly dolled and over-smiling tarts standing out front under the jacaranda trees, pulling at their stockings, waving at the taxis, and shoving with palms the bottom of their hair. Though I sensed that they all disliked me, I picked the one who seemed to dislike me the most, a "repetition compulsion" as Fasstink would've labeled it, or a subconscious method in other words to symbolically reenact the early days with my mother and get her somehow to like me so she would not leave or perhaps leave her before she could leave me. Either way there was probably something to that. She said her name was Carmelita. Squat, fleshy-cheeked, flat-nosed, and slightly cross-eyed, she looked like a *Veracruzana*. She had a gap between her teeth and smelled of four differently colored melons. She wore a red locket around her neck the size of a pocket watch. She must have been about twenty-six. I asked her if she wanted to go somewhere, a restaurant or the beach. She said *osteones*, which might have meant either, and quoted me a price. I paid her double up front out of discretionary funds, said *vamanos*, and off we went to an oyster bar that she knew of not far from the sea.

Afterward, I felt drained and ashamed and found a church, where I slumped in a pew at the back near the candles. The Virgin Mother towered gold above me. The light coming through the windows was like dust from a box of Cap'n Crunch. I thought about driving south and abandoning my truck and just living on the beach for a while. Maybe the ocean would cure me. But I had had those kinds of thoughts before and recognized them as precipitous, especially since I could not swim. So I made a quick prayer to the Mexican God who is more forgiving than the American One and went to find my truck. Maybe when I got back on my feet I would become a better man.

9.   Gigantic Australian Counterclockwise Stampedes

EVERY NIGHT I CAPPED THE *RACING FORM*, AND EVERY MORNING I checked the results in the newspaper. I'd usually have two or three winners, not all of them favorites. After about two weeks of this I drove over to the satellite facility on the Del Mar Fairgrounds to test my methods. The place was packed. It was a posh spot with plush carpet, plenty of tables and chairs, scores of televisions, and many vendors selling food, booze, and news. I recognized a few faces. No one recognized me. I would not have recognized myself either. Gravity and antipsychotics had served to pull down my heavily scarred face. I was flushed and at the same time sallow. And my nose, the only thing rigid about me, stuck out of my face like a bird beak. Trembly and disheveled, I looked like an old stressed-out Irish mariner or Barbra Streisand after electroshock therapy.

I had never been in a room with so many televisions, each one with a different picture. There were races from all over the country and all over the world, including Australia, where they ran gigantic counterclockwise fields in virtual stampedes. Though they had betting machines, I felt more comfortable at the windows, letting the live human push the buttons for me. Everyone shouting or rooting for a different race jammed my signals and I could not pick a single winner. The flickering of the television screens robbed the electricity from my brain. I switched from Santa Anita to Turfway Park and then to Hialeah but I had no luck anywhere.

Then I saw my father in the paddock at Santa Anita helping saddle up an entry in the seventh. Mercy Blast, a two-year-old, was seven to one. My father was good with first time two-year-olds, but I did not bet first-time two-year-olds, so naturally he won.

While I was watching a crazy backward Australian race, someone swatted me across the back with a program.

I turned to see a short-legged, middle-aged fellow with hickory-flecked green eyes, a nose that looked to have been broken more than once, a bit of a paunch, a deeply cleft chin, and a mangled yellow smile. He wore brown corduroys, clumpy dress boots, and a red plaid short-sleeved shirt with snap pockets.

"That you, Eddie?" he shouted in the voice of Norton on *The Honeymooners*, tipping his head over and flipping back a long strand of oiled hair that immediately dropped back into his eye. "Eddie Plum, I don't believe it."

"Shelly Hubbard," I returned.

"Man have you changed," he said, waving his program under his chin. "I wasn't even sure it was you."

No one from my ancient past would have been a more welcome sight, for Shelly was as much of a screwball and more of an outsider than I was. "You haven't changed at all," I said. "You still dealing records?"

"Oh yeah, babe, what else am I gonna do?" He looked around. "Last I heard, you were up in Frisco."

"Yeah, got married and lost my mind."

He cackled. "Shouldn'ta got married. Hey, just saw your dad. Won the seventh with Mercy Blast."

"Yeah, I didn't have that one," I said.

"Me neither. Seven to one. Sheezus."

"Still don't like the two-year-olds?"

"Not with your money. Who you like in the ninth?"

"I'm done for the day, lost thirteen in a row."

"Me too. What do you say we go get a beer somewhere?"

10. Hermaphrodites, Bikers, and French Teachers

ABOUT A MILE INLAND FROM THE TRACK, NOT FAR FROM THE SAN Dieguito River, on a hillock overlooking the marshy maritime mists of the estuary, stood Moby Dick's, a punk bar with a leviathan chipped blue-cement whale-mouth entrance. I had seen Siouxsie and the Banshees here back in 1980 before someone threw a smoke bomb and the show was canceled. Del Mar is a stodgy old town inhabited by many rich and famous geriatrics, but Dick's still attracted freaks, not only masqueraders with patches on their eyes and safety pins hanging from earlobes but ghouls, goths, hermaphrodites, bikers, and French teachers. And now and again a relic band like the Misfits or Social Distortion would parade through on their way up to L.A.

Shelly and I parked our trucks around back. Shelly fancied Japanese pickups. He'd owned a brown Datsun when I knew him before. There had been what looked like scorch marks up the passenger side door of his Datsun, which I had discounted since it was an old beat-up truck that he'd bought used, but now I saw that his newer lighter-colored Nissan pickup had the same scorch marks up the same door.

"Where you get those burn marks?" I asked him. "Been driving through hell?"

"All my life, babe," he replied, and we both slapped our hips and roared.

The sun had set and a juniper-scented fog was lapping up against the streetlamps. We entered through the whale's mouth into a large room with copper comets suspended from a green tin-shingled ceiling and many bronze statues of Ahab and Jonah in various dramatic poses, even if in the good book it says that Jonah was swallowed by a fish. Ancient graffiti remained on the brick walls: Billy Barty Traveling Death Circus.

In the foreground was an enormous glowing Wurlitzer like the pipe organ from the set of *The Phantom of the Opera*. Beyond that were three pool tables and a cavernous vault where the bands played. A dozen patrons milled about: a woman with a boa constrictor wound round her neck was lowered in conversation with a man in a tilted black beret who looked like an angry ferret. A woman dressed like one of the peafowls at Napa State was shooting pool with a topless David Bowie-type whose tattoos were so deep you could read her bones. A pallid woman in a red velveteen dress with a face like Burt Lancaster sitting four stools down gave us a muscular wink. Shelly had been born to sadistic parents, so, though he wasn't a fan of the punk scene and dressed and combed his hair as if he were still in the fourth grade, he meshed with the Moby Dick's crowd more than he would admit. He looked around, gave a nod of approval to the David Bowie lass, peeled off his jacket, draped it over the back of a stool, and climbed aboard.

Kang Soo, or Soo as she was called, the agelessly sexy, always working Korean owner of Dick's, glided up in front of us and leaned forward with a brittle smile, her elbows resting on the black leather cushion that rode the length of both sides of the long curved bar. We ordered draft pints of the house specialty, Old Asthma Attack. Soo raised dripping tankards and set them on coasters before us. Shelly rolled his eyes upward and drained the contents of his.

He wiped his mouth with the back of his hand. "How come they call it Asthma Attack?"

"It's a wheat beer," I said. "The guy who invented it I think was allergic to wheat."

"I think I'm allergic to wheat, too," he said.

"You want another one?" challenged Soo.

"Why not?" he said with a hiccup and a shrug. "Maybe I'll get lucky and my lungs will seize up." His squeaky cackle was so infectious I laughed with him. He pushed his goblet forward.

Gloomy Soo pulled him another.

As Shelly settled into his second draft, we caught up on things. He chortled and licked his lips as I recounted my Napa escapades with Sturtz, Fuckface, Boothby, Flightless, and the rest of my old straitjacket pals. "Never thought it would be *you*," he crowed. "Always thought *I'd* be the one they'd put away."

"It's never too late," I reassured him. "Tell me about yourself."

Shelly recalled the last decade and a half. Little had changed. Forty-four years old and he was still living in the same house where he was born, still single but looking, still without a draft number, a social security number, or a record with the Internal Revenue Service (his only official existence at the Department of Motor Vehicles). He was still running the same secondhand record business he'd started when he was sixteen. He still had that ruined smile from a pair of neglected teeth that had turned into a massive infection and spread from his sinuses right up into his brain, rendering him bedridden, delirious, depressed, over and improperly medicated, and in constant commute to Tijuana to see yet another Mexican dentist. He was still making regular trips to Tijuana, he said, trying to get the mess in his head straightened out.

More cups of beer arrived. Shelly drank as if he were trying to wet his face, gulping the draft back like an old prospector just in from a day of mining boron. He kept shooting me wild, guilty, suspicious glances.

I dropped two quarters into the music trivia machine planted on the bar in front of me. I figured I'd nail all the questions, but the first one stumped me. "Hey, Shell, what song did Tommy James write for Alive N Kickin'?"

Shelly, gulping now from his third Asthma Attack, took his eyes off the woman with the snake around her neck, checked himself without interest in the mirror behind the liquor bottles, and jabbed at the snapped-down flaps of his collar with his thumbs. "God my nuts hurt," he said.

"No, that wasn't it."

"I think it's my epididymis again." He grimaced and writhed on his stool like a cattle hand after a long day.

"Four seconds," I said. "You're gonna screw up my bonus."

"Tighter, Tighter," he said. "Like my epididymis."

"Thanks, don't need the subtitle."

He scowled over at the machine. "What did Bobby *Fuller* die of? Everybody knows that one. They got any *hard* questions on there?"

I pressed C. Gasoline inhalation.

Shelly was hunched over the bar now, hands folded, peering

up at me. "Should be a button for murdered." He jerked his head to clear the forelock. "Whoever he fought he lost." He slapped the bar and honked for a while like a cold engine starting, an *ee ee ee* that invited me to join in.

"Okay, Mr. Know-it-All, who was the lead singer of the Talking Heads? You don't know that one, do you?"

"No idea." His knowledge of the pop music industry from the origin of rock until about 1976 was encyclopedic. After 1976 there was an abrupt drop-off, as if the world or American culture had come to an end, which you could make an argument for.

A pasty girl dressed in black lace, hair shot and teased, her fingernails lacquered black, strolled in.

"Funeral home's down the street, Morticia," Shelly sidemouthed at me as she passed, her shoulders giving off waves of lilac and cedar.

The goth sat, ordered Southern Comfort neat, rummaged in her purse, and glanced over at us with her spidery eyes.

These children mourning the death of the republic were beyond Shelly's ken. "Looks like a corpse," he whispered to me.

"That's the idea, son."

Shelly showed that snaggled yellow smile, all the molars in it extracted or dissolved.

The goth lit a cigarette but did not inhale. She looked at me and I wondered by her expression if she could read my mind.

"She's looking at you, Gomez," Shelly gruffed with a leer. "You oughta take her home. She's probably tired of sleeping alone in the same casket."

I thought, despite the complications and the risk, about taking her home.

"Dead girls are too easy, man," I replied.

Shelly had a fantasy about finding a vulnerable woman on a beach or in a park and having his way with her, not a far cry from necrophilia, and he replied predictably, "That's about the only action I can get these days."

I sang *sotto voce*: "She's a horrible corpse but she's always a woman to me."

In the middle of a splash Shelly gasped, inhaling beer. Choking and snorting, he slapped the bar. "God, don't joke when I'm on the intake, babe," he mouthed in an odd inflection like a poor immigrant yelling at his wife. "I just about dropped my prostate gland there."

"Go ahead and drop it, babe," I replied. "What do you need one for anyway?"

Shelly, still relishing the exchange and the novelty of a necrophilic tumble, wriggled on his stool, as if testing his prostate. "I think I felt it work loose there." His gaze swept the floor and he tongued his Tijuana smile. "Maybe it was my epididymis."

We were both chirping and giggling now like schoolgirls between wisecracks. I had earned my bonus on the trivia machine but lost interest in a second round. The goth with her Southern Comfort and the freaks in their snakes and green feather gossamer and Ziggy Stardust tattoos glanced over at our gigglefest with vague distaste. Soo watched us stone-faced but ready to smile if duty called. Shelly splashed the beer against his face and somehow gulped it down.

"Let's go to Santa Anita tomorrow, babe," I said.

"What are you talkin' about, babe?" he chided, turning on me and speaking in the angry immigrant voice. "You wanna drive all the way up to L.A.? What do you think they got satellite for?"

"Satellite's the Tower of Babel," I said. "I need to smell those horses and see their flesh."

He fingered back his oiled, side-parted hair and regarded me as the devout regards the infidel.

"Probably going to rain anyway," I added with a shrug.

"Rain," he whispered, narrowing his eyes, for rain is rare enough in southern California that it has meaning: it means that pace models collapse, morning lines dissolve, turf races are moved to dirt, fields shrink. It means, to the astute player, a man who might study and circle and cipher a *Racing Form* all night, as if it were some kind of sacred text, or more precisely because he has no other life to speak of, the possibility of opportunity.

"Tell you what," I said. "I'll swing by your place around ten and if you want to go, fine. If not, I'll tell 'em your prostate fell out."

"I don't need a prostate to bet, do I?" he retorted, taking a slop from his tankard. "Is it a betting gland? No wonder I'm doing so lousy. Tell you what, babe, I'll go with you."

11.   Coco Puff

AT TEN THE NEXT MORNING I PARKED IN FRONT OF SHELLY'S dark, suburban ranch-style tract home built somewhere in the middle of the twentieth century. Like Shelly, it hadn't changed much. In our days together long ago I'd picked him up and dropped him off here countless times, but he'd never invited me inside. I'd never even been past the front gate. He routinely referred to his sadistic parents as "Nazis," but he was so secretive and kept his life so carefully partitioned that it took me years to learn the grim details: that his mother and father dressed him in girls' clothes, made him eat without utensils, twice killed his pets as punishment, and kept him in a cage in the garage with a bowl of water like a dog. It was a forbidding, peeling old house, the kind the kids would skip on Halloween night, the kind you'd dare your childhood friends to peek in the window of or knock on its door.

Shelly was habitually late. Untold times in the days of our youth he'd stated an intention to meet me somewhere and never shown, or he'd actually follow me from the track or the fast-food joint to some agreed-upon destination and then peel away into the night before we arrived. He suffered from a variety of maladies, malaises, manqués, and melancholias, imaginary and otherwise. He harbored so many secrets I don't think he could keep track of them all. I asked him once why he kept so many secrets and he replied with a leer, "How do you think I *survive*, babe?" His appearance at my front door when I had that apartment on University Avenue two decades before, six pack in hand, was almost always unannounced. And though he might stay for several hours, pondering an elusive God or delving into mare cycles and pace configurations, he usually left abruptly, sometimes mid-sentence, as if fearful of that sweep of the hour hand that would trigger within him some unholy change. One of the many questions about Shelly that I could not answer was why he still lived with these people who had tortured and disabled him.

I took a sip from the cup of coffee I'd bought at the 7-Eleven and puzzled over the third race: ten-thousand-dollar claimers that'd raced against each other for the last three years in mixed fields at three different tracks and each time a different horse had won. I'd seen and written about this type of contest so many times I felt I should know the outcome. "The race is not always to the swift," wrote Damon Runyon, "but that is the way to bet it." Except horses are herd animals, obliged to natural pecking orders, which means that a faster horse will often defer to its deemed superior. This is the basis of the concept of class, the crux of class-speed continuum analysis, and why the Plum Variable is a useful handicapping tool, as it automatically sorts fields and adjusts class values pertinent to the track you're playing. Still, the codes of primodromes such as Santa Anita, Del Mar, Saratoga, and Belmont Park are the hardest to crack because, unlike the mezzodromes and the llamadromes, the quality of competition prevents too many of the entrants in the field from being eliminated.

At a cheap-purse track, with inferior animals of dubious fitness assembled from diverse tracks, speed (the fastest horse) will prevail 90 percent of the time. At a middle-purse track, as the quality of stock and racing conditions improve, the percentage falls to 50. High purse tracks are all about class (algorithmically determined from pedigree, overall record, and average winnings measured against status versus contenders), so I didn't concern myself with which horse had the best off-track record, neither did I care who was wearing mud caulks, had switched to blinkers or Lasix, or which had the best closing fractions. At the primodrome I ignore Beyer figures and workouts, except as an indication of fitness and form. All things considered, it's usually the best animal, the dominant-superior of its group, the owner of the highest Plum Variable, that wins these contests, if the break isn't too bad, if the field isn't too large, if the trainer doesn't tell the jockey to go easy, if the meds are right, if it isn't raining, if if if.

I thought back to the day before at Del Mar satellite. Though I'd lost all thirteen races, I'd not handicapped badly. Most of my horses had hit the board, and the ones that had run out had gotten boxed in or pinched or had bobbled at the start, or the jockey hadn't switched leads, or the battery in his buzzer was dead down the stretch, or he was hungover or blowing kisses to his sweetheart in the grandstand as he passed. Even when you're playing and handicapping well you need luck to win.

And I knew I was going to win soon. Bring someone who knows nothing about horses to the track and usually they win. Flip a coin enough times. Bet the number two in every race. You can't win them all, but you can't lose them all either.

It was a sunny day in a quiet decaying middle-class neighborhood in the dappled shade of overgrown trees. My radio was off and staring at the third race I felt myself about to have a moment of prescience when someone knocked on my window. Startled, I looked over to see Shelly Hubbard, hank of balmed hair dropped into his face, Racing Form rolled and tucked under his arm, pen riding on his ear.

I wound my window down.

"Where's the rain, babe?" he said, glancing up at the blue sky.

"In Spain," I replied.

"I didn't hear you drive up," he said.

"Climb on in, son, unless you're going to clean my windshield. You want to make the first race?"

He climbed on in, some sort of tissue-wrapped fast-food or gas-station sandwich in one hand, a styro cup of coffee in the other. He arranged his Form on the dashboard. He smelled in close quarters of mushrooms on toast.

I pulled out onto the boulevard, careful to observe all the traffic laws except for the feint I made at a squirrel that ran out in front of me. Sunday morning quiet. I turned on the radio and found it tuned to the NPR station and *Prairie Home Companion*, *Hee-Haw* for liberals, as my fellow inmate Sturtz liked to call it, so I pushed the buttons until I found an oldies station. Shelly knew the words to every song; he knew the name of the frontman, the history, the songwriter, the B-side, what label it was on. He'd say Chess records or Columbia, A&M or Roulette, Starlites on Peak records, Miracles on Standard Groove. He'd recite numbers, anecdotes, dates. Personally, he admired Brian Wilson, Ricky Nelson, and those doo-wop kings the Flamingoes. His most valuable record, a mint copy of "Rocket 88," worth about five thousand dollars, he bought at a garage sale for a quarter. What was notable about the way he listened to music was that he seemed to take no pleasure from it, no singing along or tapping his foot, no snapping of fingers or bobbing of the head. I'd seen him in action on his record-buying circuits many times: his evaluation of a record was based strictly upon authenticity and condition. Possession diminishes passion, as any married person will tell you, or in other words, once something you love becomes your job, it's not quite as much fun.

We drove along the ocean for a while, the view that draws so many to stay.

"I feel like a turd today," Shelly said.

"Too many brewskis," I replied.

"Had about seven more after you left." He took a bite of his sandwich. "This is what I was wondering last night when I couldn't sleep. After all those years in the bughouse, do you still believe in God?"

"I do."

He seemed upset, as if I'd given the wrong answer. "After all the shit they put you through?"

"Look, man, I've seen him."

"At the laughing academy."

"Without spirit," I said, "matter is just a blob."

"With Steve McQueen." He cackled for a while, getting teary eyed, then he wiped his eyes with his forearm and said earnestly, "Wish I could believe in God."

"You know what we forgot to talk about last night?"

He got a gulp from his coffee. "What's that?"

"Your love life."

"Love life," he roared.

"Ever since I've known you you've had a honey on the line."

Shelly brightened, finger combed his hair, pleased that I would ask. "Well, I have been seeing this waitress every Tuesday for the last year or so."

"You're dating her?"

"Well, I go to the restaurant where she works."

"You ask her out yet?"

Not having had the benefit of a normal family, and believing there was such a thing, Shelly relied heavily on television for instruction on how everyone else, the "lucky people" in his view, lived. Television also provided the basis for many of his identities. Most of the time he was David Janssen in *The Fugitive*, a hardcore covert loner misunderstood, estranged by fate from the comforts that most Americans take for granted. But now he was Bud from the family sitcom *Father Knows Best*, whipping back his hair. He finished the sandwich, balled up the wrapping, set it next to him on the seat. "Not yet."

The rules were we couldn't go too deeply into Shelly's girlfriends, only his intentions with them, which was dating and eventual marriage and Jane Wyman scenes with tinkling martini glasses glittering with the dry vermouth of ideal love. In the few years I'd known him before I'd moved to the Bay Area he had described many of his love interests to me: an unidentified TV news personality, the wife of an unspecified friend, a go-go dancer, a barmaid, a cashier at a grocery store, a neighbor, a girl he met one night walking along Harbor Island. I'd never met or even caught a glimpse of any of these women and he'd never produced a grain of evidence that any had ever existed. Pressing him for specifics would only make him recede, so it was a game we played on the shallowest levels, like thirdgraders giggling about girls on the playground. Still, it was a long drive and, curious, I continued to probe into his fancy. "She married, your Coco's girl?"

"How'd you know she worked at Coco's?"

"You told me."

"No I didn't."

"Okay. I guessed. I know it's your favorite restaurant."

"It's not my favorite restaurant."

"She married, your Coco Puff?"

"Divorced."

"Really? Kids?"

"Two boys."

"Interesting. "How old are they?"

"Not sure. One's in college."

"State?"

"Pepperdine."

Good detail. Maybe the girl was real. "So she must be around forty."

He bunched his lips, nodded for a while. An Italian sports car, flat black and all fiberglass, blasted past on the left with a *zzzshiiiing*. This was hardly fantasy territory. I considered: forty-year-old Coco's waitress, divorced mother of two. "What's her name, anyway?" He scrubbed his eyelid with a pinkie, offered a half smile that might've been chagrin but was probably closer to *I've Got a Secret*. We both knew he wasn't going to tell me. The names and locations of his girlfriends were always concealed.

Shelly was fascinated with the black actress Roxie Roker, who played neighbor Helen Willis on *The Jeffersons*. Helen Willis's husband was white, making this the first regular prime-time show to feature an interracial couple. Roxie was also the real-life mother of multiple-Grammy-award-winning musician Lenny Kravitz, whose father was white. Shelly's whole suburban life had been as white as Pat Boone's 1957 B-side single "The Wang Dang Taffy-Apple Tango (Mambo Cha Cha Cha)," a song he detested, but black was the very soul of all the music he admired and sought, so it was no surprise when he confessed to me once with a breathily anxious giggle that he'd been in love for many years with Motown diva and frontwoman for the Supremes, Miss Diana Ross.

I decided to loosen him with a little levity. "She's black, right?" He let out a squeaky laugh that was almost a cry. His green eyes glittered.

"Hey, maybe we can double date. You bring the black chick, I'll bring the dead one."

He jiggled from laughter. He had to crack his window an inch. He seemed to be having trouble getting air. It was all this talk about women and love that made him breathless.

"Babe, babe, babe." I assumed my psychiatric voice, calm but firm, trying to shake his carousel of imps, poses, and caricatures and get to the bottom of his girlfriend. "How can we have a serious discussion about someone you care about if I don't even know her name?"

"Deborah," he blurted, grinning wildly, showing off his wrecked and gapped smile, his eyes swinging side to side.

"Where does she live?"

He wagged his finger at me. I was getting too close.

A CHP unit zipped past us on the left, emergency top lights blazing.

"I need to know what to put on the wedding invitations," I said.

He barked a laugh, his eyes widened in terror, and he was replaced by a more somber version of himself. Whenever he shifted like this I was reminded of his insistence that he had a multiple personality disorder, that he might be seven or eight, maybe twenty or two hundred distinct personalities, each independent and unaware of its neighbor.

It was difficult to read his thoughts, there were so many curtains and walls and infested vapors I doubted that he knew what the truth about himself was. I had granted him the overworked phenomenon called "compartmentalization," a theoretical process by which the essential personality is fractured through a series of traumatic events in childhood. This theory is also sometimes applied as an explanation of the operation of habitual, recreational killers. Note also the Russian and American Cold War experiments to create "super agents" by similar processes, especially the CIA's MKUltra mind-control programs, which may or may not have produced brainwashed patsy assassins such as Sirhan Sirhan. Create a genuine multiple personality disorder and you have an agent who can operate indefinitely without remorse or memory of the deed. In the case of Shelly, however, I'd never seen evidence to confirm that one personality was not aware of what another was thinking or doing or had thought or done. Raised by the television, it seemed more likely that these "personalities" were simply assimilations of TV characters he admired from the 1960s.

I didn't doubt for a second the accounts of his sadistic upbringing. Still, it seemed that too much of his self-perception relied on being an outsider raised by cruel parents. He also read too many shaky and sordid pop-psych bestsellers such as *Sybil*. He didn't realize that most of us are formed by stress and pain, most of us perceive ourselves as outsiders, most of us have suffered major parental failures, most of us have felt crazy or broken down or on the brink of yodeling off into the night, and that most of us lead multiple lives.

I had to slow for an accident up ahead. Shelly stared at the once graceful, now mangled black Lamborghini. The driver, as far as I could tell, was still inside. Five miles down the way, in a dream voice, he said the same thing he always said when we talked about his imaginary girlfriends. "Where do you think I should take her?"

"Does she like the horses?"

"Hmmm," he said, as if this had never occurred to him.

"Movies are good, too," I offered. "You don't have to find out how truly incompatible you are for a couple of hours."

He raised an eyebrow at me and shook open his *Form*, squinting at the numbers, then looking down at the radio as if it were transmitting alien signals. He said, "Who you like in the first?"

12. Marvelous Marvelle / Let the Sunshine In

SANTA ANITA WAS THE MOST ELEGANT OF THE THREE MAJOR southern California racetracks. Hollywood Park, with similar purse structures and a nearly identical list of competing jockeys, trainers, and owners, sat in a bad part of town and had none of the glitz of its sister to the north. Del Mar will always be my favorite—intimate, foggy, right on the ocean, its season short-lived as happiness, the ghost of Bing Crosby crooning the rinky-dink jingle "Where the Turf Meets the Surf" before the start of each card. Santa Anita didn't have the atmosphere of Del Mar, but they'd dumped the cash in: Clydesdales, cobblestone, a panoramic view of the San Gabriel mountains, even a guy with a long-necked bugle announcing the post parade.

Santa Anita, Del Mar, and Hollywood Park were on a circuit in those days (the track at Hollywood Park has since gone dark) and there were many people—jockeys, trainers, clockers, grooms, vendors, waiters, and margarita girls—who followed that circuit to make their livings. The three tracks took turns throughout the year, never running contemporaneously. Many bettors would follow this circuit as well and we'd nod or wave or exchange a few words with a familiar face. Though Shelly was socially facile, he became reticent around those he did not know well or trust, fearing that they might steal and undeservedly benefit from his hard-won knowledge and the fruits of his research. For many years Hollywood Park had a special Thanksgiving card: a free turkey dinner with admission, a sad feast with all the misfit gamblers who sought on this day not those they loved but to wring a few more precious drops from their adrenal glands. Shelly and I had attended three of these cheerless Styrofoam-tray repasts. My father, I would lay heavy odds, never missed a single one.

Shelly and I didn't look for a place to sit or camp. We had to move, Shelly getting more and more excited as the first post approached. He threw his *Form* over a concession table, took the pen down off his ear, and made a quick inspection of his previous night's calculations. A slow transformation began, as if fire ants were replacing the iron molecules in his red blood cells. "Bet some doubles today?"

"Yowp."

"Who you want in the first?"

"I like 'em all except the favorite and the Chilean shipper from Bay Meadows."

"Favorite off eight days." He smacked his program. "Hasn't won twice in a row for three years."

"Front wraps, too," I added. "*Digest* marked them off last time out."

Significant eyebrow work of the gambling addict here. Throw out the lame favorite and you're getting somewhere. Shelly was about to drool. He jerked his head and threw that stray lock back. "And roll some pick threes. You want to split a few?"

"I'm up."

His eyes flicked wider and wider, the fluid in his joints warming to blend with his saliva. "A pick six?"

"They got the one-handed betting machines in the bathrooms if you want to get rid of your money fast, babe."

He nodded at me as if he were sucking on a funny-tasting gum drop. He wanted to bet bet bet bet, but he knew I was right. To have a crack at winning a pick six you need a multiple base ticket investment of at least $128, and once you've outlaid that much with your actual odds of hitting six races in a row still somewhere around a million to one, it's a lit match to your cash. The challenge of the game was what mattered to us. Money was simply the method of keeping score.

The bugler came out at twelve minutes to post and I ambled down to the rail to have a look at the horses in the first race, examining coats, eyes, ears, and looking for neck and kidney sweat. As soon as I saw the Chilean shipper, Mata Morose, I knew he would win. His ears were pricked, his coat shone, and he was pumped up and almost nuts that the trainer had given him some M&M's, the colored shells of which were still stuck in his teeth.

I ran back up and told Shelly I thought the Chilean shipper would win. He looked at me as if I'd lost my mind. We argued, but I couldn't say, until long after we'd cashed our winning tickets that Mata Morose loved M&M's because M&M's had caffeine, a prohibited substance and a distinct and unfair advantage. The horse would probably be disqualified after its mandatory urine test. Mata Morose was 36-1, meaning he would pay thirty-six times the unit you bet on him (plus your bet back, making a two-dollar wager worth seventy-four dollars if he won). I left Shelly shaking his head and ran to the window, where I bet five dollars on the nose (to win) thirty seconds before the race went off.

Mata Morose won wire-to-wire by five.

"How did you know that?" Shelly demanded, staring at me angrily.

"Hunch," I answered.

Shelly believed in the *Form* as if it were some kind of laboratory-certified navigational instrument and had to run his finger down the columns again to see where he'd miscalculated. The problem with the *Form* player is he's going to catch very few longshots. After he weighs the numbers, enters his pace model, considers the Plum and the Beyer, jockey changes, bleeder medication, weight, age, morning workouts, and the rest of it, he's going to come up pretty much with the same horse that everyone else using a Racing Form has. The guy who sets the morning line is a *Form* player too. Only granny here with her bridge club betting her grandson's age and the guy who's spent the last decade and a half in a mental institution and developed through blindness, head trauma, dreams, drugs, and deprivation a heightened perception of reality is going to nail the Chilean shipper from Bay Meadows.

"Yeah?" said Shelly, shoving out his chin. "All right, who you like in the second then?"

"Don't know yet." I had circled Red Freak Wanna Ride, but the game had changed. "I gotta look."

Shelly had an excellent memory and knew his bloodlines, the successful dams and sires all the way back to the triple-crown-winner Whirlaway. His conservative style of play had not wavered in twenty years so that year in and year out he was close to a break-even player, grinding along from favorite to favorite. He muttered, frowned, and dragged around squinting at the *Racing Form* trying to figure how he could fit the newly acquired information into the next race. Was the rail dead? Was it going to be a longshot day? Were Bay Meadows shippers suddenly viable? Should he just go flush all his money down the toilet now?

In the next race, for fillies and mares five years old or under who had not won two races in their career, Shelly glowered at me doubtfully, wondering if I'd pull another rabbit out of my hat. I was going back and forth between Red Freak Wanna Ride, the eight horse, and Silly Pilgrim, the six, until all of a sudden I heard the one, River Shannon, say, "When I get back I'll have carrots and apples," which is what my father always gave his winners (the losers got Purina and hay). And though it wasn't my father's horse, I said, "I think it's River Shannon."

Shelly smacked his program indignantly and said, "How? Thing hasn't won in two years."

"Just a feeling," I said coyly. "Call it carrots and apples."

The elderly woman in front of us, who'd also gotten Mata Morose in the previous race on a number coinciding with her grandson's age, beamed at us. "I've got River Shannon, too."

Shelly, thinking he'd nail the first fifty-to-one shot of his life with the help of a recovering schizophrenic and a doddering grandmother, reluctantly joined our cause and volunteered to roll it into some pick threes.

River Shannon couldn't get out of the gate, and though she made a valiant dash on the grandstand turn she lugged out wide in the stretch and finished eighth in a field of nine. Shelly smoldered.

I said, "Hey look, it's been a while since I've done this."

"Carrots and apples," he grumbled.

I decided that unless something really beamed out at me I'd better lower my antennae and stick to the *Form*, and if we lost then at least Shelly would be satisfied that I had violated no sacred conventions and we would remain friends.

"You gonna go see your Dad?" he asked.

"Probably not. What'll he say? Deadbeat crackpot with a dead guy's driver's license betting longshots. He hates people like that. It's better he doesn't know I'm here."

Shelly prized that kind of self-effacing talk and not only forgave me but was once again on my side. "We'll hit the pick six," he declared. "That'll show him."

Down on the tarmac below, a group of drunken rural stereotypes, three men and two ladies, sitting on a blanket, had begun to argue. The men wore tight pants that showed long stretches of white sockless ankle. The ladies had piled-high hair, and one wore a low-cut white blouse splashed with red hearts. A ruckus started up and a chair was broken. One of the men lurched up and a beer bottle flew. The crowd receded, giving them room. Punches ensued. The men scrabbled across the pavement through the trash grunting and trying to tear off each other's shirts, their white ankles flashing, while the women rooted them on. Many spectators laughed and applauded as if bumpkin scuffles were a regular feature between the second and third race. Security arrived and the three men and one lady were taken away. One of the fellows was badly cut, his face glazed in blood. The woman with the unbuttoned heart blouse, the only one remaining after the melee, stared at Shelly, her glossy open mouth like a tunnel in an amusement park ride.

"Gosh," Shelly said. "I wonder if we should take her home."

It began to rain then, just a sifting at first and then the wind started to blow the pop cups in a waxy clatter and the seagulls began to bounce on the currents and that harbor smell lifted from the ground and the raindrops began to swell and splat. The crowd standing out in the open made a few collar adjustments. A few tugged at cap bills. When the rain came in earnest everyone scattered for cover.

Shelly and I stood at the edge of the overhang, studying the oddsboard, waiting for the post parade, watching the track surface go from fast to slow to muddy. A sloppy track is like a fast track because the dirt is near liquid and hooves can find purchase on the hard surface underneath, but a muddy track is like running in mashed potatoes. Mud and slop are two different, nearly opposite, factorial worlds. We waited for the announcement to see whether our decision should be based upon slop or mud. Two minutes before the second race the track was deemed "sloppy." Shelly and I looked at each other and nodded.

For weeks you lose. You get close, you catch bad breaks, you fall a nose short in a photo, your horse breaks down, the inquiry sign goes up and they take your number off the board. The gods chuckle and it sounds

like the wind and the madness and futility of your life. You couldn't pick
a horse if it crawled up your nose. Seagulls shit on your head. You want to
tear your program to bits. You want to throw your money in the air. You
want to go home and get drunk. You want to crawl back into your hospital
bed or shoot yourself in the brain.

But then, without warning, you start hitting winners, and it
doesn't matter if you can hear the horses talk or see two minutes and eighteen seconds ahead of everyone else, or if you pick numbers randomly or
eavesdrop on granny or continue to refine faithfully your antiquated system. You are going to win.

Shelly and I knew how to play the primodrome on a gumbo
track in the rain. We looked for horses with a little step, those who were
not afraid of slipping in the slop. The outside posts were virtually dead.
The speed was holding. Shelly knew the complete history of nearly every
animal competing. In one glance, as if we were playing a mezzodrome, we
could eliminate half the field or more. The harder it rained, the shorter
the fields got.

Rain prickled along the asphalt; the sky was low and rumbling
gray. Sleek, thundering mud-coated beasts rose out of the mist, and each
time, though you could barely read the numbers on the twisted and splat-
tered saddlecloths as they streaked past, it was the right number. It was
magic time. Shelly and I shouted and danced and slapped the high flesh,
sharing the sweet endocrine blossom of victory.

We hit our first pick three and split the cash, eighty-six each.
The cameramen up in the press box taping for the TV recap tonight had
already cut to us twice. Shelly became so transported, so ecstatic, he drifted away, standing in the deluge, shouting like Brando in *Streetcar*, boots
steaming, face raised to the sky, completely ignoring the wet hillbilly in
the red-heart blouse who adored him. *Come on, Laffit, bring it on, Laffit
Baby, atta baby.*

My father's horse, a bay gelding named Chiquilla Vanilla, got
the four hole in the sixth race at six to one. Everything on grass had been
moved to dirt. Normally a turf horse, Chiquilla Vanilla was the longest shot
on the board, even if there were only four horses in the field. I knew what
a nightmare this was for my father, who loved and took care of his animals
better than the people in his life. He had enough money that he could've

scratched all his entries and not risked injury to them, but even he wouldn't admit that he was a gambler too. Chiquilla Vanilla won going away. Shelly and I slammed the high fives and toddled off to buy another round.

At the beer booth Shelly made a joke to the girl who drew our two jumbo Michelobs. He flashed his mangled smile and said to me as he handed me my cup, "I oughta ask her out. She's a margarita girl at Del Mar."

And he would've asked her out, too, he really would've, right there on the spot, lived happily ever after with a margarita girl—maybe she could've gotten me a date too and we could have had a double margarita marriage—but the seventh race was coming. There were only three races left and when would the magic come again? We needed to bear down. Shelly threw his *Form* open across a concession table and commenced to decipher the next race, nearly panting as he worked the numbers, the pages so wet they should've torn from the point of his pen, but he was in a trance state, invincible, still speaking in the angry immigrant voice. "I'm like Marilyn Monroe, baby," he crowed. "Get on me while I'm hot."

It was still raining hard at the end of the ninth race. The park was almost empty. Soaked to the skin, we scurried across the empty parking lot toward my truck. "Goddamnit," he said. "I toldya we shoulda bet the pick six. We woulda won!"

I was about to remind him that the pick six had been canceled when a woman called to us.

We turned. It was the mountain girl in the heart blouse. "Can y'all give me a ride home?" she called.

"Where you live?" I yelled back

"Downey," she said, moving toward us, her breasts lifting and falling splendidly against all those wet and shiny hearts. "It's just down the road apiece."

Despite being slack-jawed and wearing a baffled expression, she was a luscious looking creature, especially now with her hair flattened by the rain and her makeup washed away. She wore a jeweled anklet and her white knee-length skirt was so wet you could see straight through it. She looked to be in her mid-twenties. "Come along then," I shouted.

"Mah name's Marvelle," she said, out of breath. And when she flashed those legs and white breasts climbing into the truck I thought about chucking it all.

"This is Shelly here," I said, "and I'm Eddie."

Shelly still standing there dripping contentedly in the rain suddenly looked four feet tall. We got ourselves arranged in the cab. The truck had a floor shift and my arm hovered above the lovely warmth of Marvelle's knees. I turned on the heater, the radio, and the wipers. It began to rain harder, the drops clanging like ball bearings on the metal roof. The seat was vinyl and the water from our wet clothes pooled under us as the windows began to fog. Above Marvelle's brown bread scent was a hint of Violet Simplicity, a perfume one of my stepmothers had worn.

"So, what happened to all your friends?" I asked her.

"They got arrest-it." She said it like a question, slinging her jaw to the left. "And Booey, he didn't do nuthin."

Shelly grinned like an eight-year-old at a peep show. "Seemed like Booey was gettin' in his licks," he said. It was funny how easily he had slipped into her accent.

I put it in gear and headed for the gate, passing some poor old tout in a clear green rain parka holding up a fan of tomorrow's winning tip sheets.

"So, how'd you all do?" she asked. "Every time I looked over you was jumpin' and whoopin' up a storm."

"We did all right," I said.

"You got a system?"

"I'm telepathic."

"No," she said. "Can you read mah mind?"

"I might," I said.

A bead of water dripped from the tip of her nose. "What am I thinkin'?"

"You wouldn't want me to say it aloud."

"Why, that is a fact."

"He's a mental patient," said Shelly.

"Oh, well, *then*," said Marvelle with a flop of the wrist.

"His father is Calvin Plum," Shelly added.

"Should I know him?"

"It isn't important," I said.

"Can you do astrology?"

"Only when the moon is in the seventh house," I said.

"And Jupiter aligns with Mars," said a grinning Shelly, who had positioned himself for the best view down her blouse. Marvelle didn't seem to mind.

"Y'all are from Mars," she said good naturedly.

A wet woman smells like a wet cat, or maybe it was Shelly, but there was that Violet Simplicity mingled in with other robust and more titillating carnal and fresh-baked lipstick scents and I got to thinking about how things take form, and I wondered what flesh really was and how it got that way and what kept it together and how it stayed so sweet and firm and why it had to decay and then re-form somehow all ripe again like a peach on the bones of its next temporary owner.

Marvelle liked to talk, and though I wasn't getting it all, Shelly was hanging on her every word.

"I don't know how I'm gonna raise bail," she was saying. "That's the third time this month. Booey and Fred just don't git along." She turned her head to each of us, giving an imploring look with those gorgeous big eyes that brought to mind a starving child. "Sometimes I think about goin' out on mah own."

"How long you been in California?" I asked

She fingered her chin. "About a year. Booey, he just got offa parole."

"Parole for what?" I said.

She turned her head haughtily. "You have to read mah mind."

"Aggravated assault."

"Anybody could've guessed that."

Shelly leered. I changed lanes and passed an old woman creeping along in her winged black Cadillac through the downpour at forty-five miles an hour, her sloshing tires half submerged. It was raining so hard I couldn't see more than a hundred yards in front of me. The wipers slung the rain side to side as an Elton John song came on the radio, "Where to Now, St. Peter?" Marvelle sang some of the words, hitting the high notes just right on "blue canoe" and "half enchanted," then found a comb and began to drag the water out of her hair.

It was twenty miles or so down the freeway to Downey. Marvelle lived on Cole Street in a rococo mansion with twenty-foot gilded pillars and a Louis XIV deck sitting atop a three-car garage. "Jesus," Shelly whispered, thinking as I had that we'd be dropping Marvelle off at a trailer park. Shelly got out and held the truck door open for her. "Thank you kindly," she said with a bow so low it would take Shelly half an hour to get that expression off his face.

We watched her stroll up the long driveway in the rain, the sodden, transparent skirt clinging to her hips. At the door, in the shelter of her portico, she gazed back at us, finger crooked on bottom lip. Shelly stared without breathing as if he were a toddler watching his mom boarding a rocket ship to another star. Finally, I waved, shoved the truck into first, and puttered away.

13.   Sex and Murder Self-Help Book

IT WAS ALMOST NINE BY THE TIME WE GOT BACK TO SAN DIEGO. Driving half-drunk in the rain on the interstate with over a thousand dollars of winnings in my pocket and Marvelle's scent like mental illness still hanging in the cab had pitched me into a swivet that would last me the week, I reckoned, unless a cop pulled me over or I got in a wreck. But I had to be positive and honest with myself and all that stuff that Doc Jangler had said. Seeing meat shop pictures of police lineups and half-naked chases across motel parking lots, I was glad I'd been able to resist Marvelle.

"We shoulda took her somewhere," Shelly said for the third time.

"And done what with her?"

"I don't know. Talked with her. Got some beer. Got a motel or something. Damn. How many opportunities do you get like that? She was beautiful."

"Well, I like to think about consequences now and again."

"Consequences!" he roared. "Since when?"

"Since Booey just got out on parole."

"Hell." Shelly groaned and shook his head heavily. "Booey'da never found us."

"Well, she's gone now, sport. You had your chance. You coulda said something."

"I figured *you'd* know what to do. You're the expert on women."

"Expert screw-up. I'll tell you what. I have *known* many a Marvelle and every one was a train wreck."

"I shoulda stayed in Downey," he whined.

"I'll take you back if you want," I said.

He shook his head. "No. It's too late. God, I wonder what she's doing now. In her bathrobe probably."

Shelly was crestfallen. Much of this I suspected was frustration that his fantasies were never realized. "We'll go back up there next week and check on her if you want," I consoled. "Booey'll probably be back in the pen by then."

This seemed to lift his mood. "You wanna beer?" he said

"Parky's still around?" I said, thinking he meant the old folks bar down the street where we had logged many an hour.

"I got some beers at my house," he said, looking over at me with a face unnervingly transparent and fragile. "You wanna come over?"

"To your *house*?" I repeated.

"Hate to see the day end," he said. "You've never been inside before, have you?"

Not in the entire time I've known you, brother, I managed to avoid saying. As much as I liked Shelly and was curious to see what his living quarters looked like, I wasn't sure I was quite up for it right now.

I parked and climbed out of the truck, my tongue tasting of dark rum, my hands tingling from holding the steering wheel tightly for too long, and followed Shelly up his driveway. Through the tall ragged hedge I caught a glimpse of a wagon wheel crawling with vines. The windows of Shelly's house were black and gleaming as obsidian. Forming a vast umbrella over the roof was an acacia tree that looked as if it had been drawn by a demonic magician with a charcoal pencil who'd then smudged the lines.

Shelly, waiting for me, keys in hand, seemed now to be having second thoughts about his invitation. Cold phantom flashes whispered through my bones. This was the house full of crazy secrets, the museum of the savior of his wretched affliction. I caught a corner-eye glimpse of his father sodomizing him in SS boots while his mother chanted in circles all around him holding an incense burner and a pattern for a size-nine dress.

Shelly pulled a string with a wooden ball attached to it. The tall wooden gate opened with a creak. "Scene of the crime," he said with a leer.

The garage was to the right, so stuffed with junk that a car could not be parked inside. The backyard was a bosky snarl of stunted pepper trees and yucca plants, thornapple, gnarled live oak, and that otherworldly acacia tree.

Besides being a repository of suffering and his sanctum of television and light beer, this is where he ran his record business, most of which involved rare or odd issue records, though he made the bulk of his earnings buying chaff like Pat Boone and Ed Ames albums and selling them at a 1,000–1,200 percent markup to the Norwegians and Japanese, the International Schlock Market as he liked to call it. Shelly hunched up in the darkness worked keys into two locks until he freed the door.

The house smelled dank, the airless chill of a vault. My impulse was to move about and open windows. He switched on the living room light. The low-pile carpet, once green, was worn down in most places to gray thread. The curtains slowly moldering to dust didn't look like they'd been opened for years. Every furnished surface in that living room was heaped with mail, *Racing Forms*, newspapers, album covers and sleeves, receipts and music lists, slumped and slid and lapping up against the island of the hallowed TV, an ancient Zenith with a curved screen. He made his way down a narrow path and turned the TV on.

Indistinct cottony green and murky blue shapes flittered and floated up into view. The speaker was about an inch wide and the voices all came across like mice playing kazoos.

"After all these years, why did you invite me in?" I asked him.

"I always wanted to invite you in before, babe. But Hitler's henchmen were here."

"Where are they now?" I said.

He cranked out one of those snaggly bugcatcher smiles. "Bay Minette."

"Alabama?"

"Yeah. They don't come back here anymore. Too old. They never much liked California anyway." He smiled without showing teeth. "I'm the sole curator of the museum now."

"When was the last time you went back?"

"Oh hell," he said, the corners of his eyes crinkling in a grimace of grievous amusement. "Twenty years maybe. Not long enough. Beer?"

"Sure thing."

He moved to the dingy gray-green *film noir* kitchen, cracked the fridge, leaned inside. I scanned the acres of spider silk strung across the ceiling.

He handed me a can of Miller Lite, shook his heavy head. The forelock, limp from a day of action in the rain, fell into his eye and he brushed it aside. "Have a seat."

I sank into the one spot open on the couch among the peanut shells and crumbling foam rubber. The end table had a stack of books, true crime and pop psychology. Shelly was a serial killer scholar. He could recite facts about the lives of Ed Gein (the real-life killer used as the model in *Psycho*) and Jeffrey Dahmer (one of the rare killers who preyed exclusively upon and cannibalized young men) with the same facility and lip-smacking relish as he could the history of early rock music. He was a fan of the famous ones as well as the obscure. His favorite might've been Charles Starkweather, a James Dean knockoff who did his work in the late fifties, was executed in 1959, and became the literary basis, as did Ed Gein, for many dramatic and creative works. Starkweather was one more case of a young misfit who got his revenge on a society that treated him poorly and refused to understand him. Shelly identified with the serial killer. I would go as far as saying that he idolized them. They seemed to him an answer. He was fond of saying with a gleam in his eye that the killer was always the last person anyone in the neighborhood suspected. I had shared this romantic view until I'd actually met and interacted with mass murderers at Napa. There was nothing glamorous about them.

Shelly pulled up a chair at a dining room table piled high with papers. There was an electric typewriter on it along with a number of records, slips, boxes, a roll of bubble wrap, and postal equipment, including a scale.

I riffled the pages of a paperback called *I Ain't Much, Baby—But I'm All I've Got*. It was well thumbed, busted binding, many underlines. It looked like the typical self-help book written by the typical screwed-up psychiatrist.

"You can read it if you want," Shelly said. "That book saved my life. It's my Bible."

"Maybe I oughta write one of these things," I said, setting the book aside. "*I Ain't Much—But at Least I Ain't Killed Myself Yet*."

Shelly's cackle punctuated the air.

"I'm serious, man," I said. "If this yo-yo can write one, why can't I?"

Shelly, taking fast sips from his beer, said, "Self-help shelves are pretty crowded."

"I've got an angle. A murder self-help book. Just kill all the people who made you feel bad. That would sell."

Shelly, sipping faster and faster, seemed to be drinking my words as well. I heard the rattle of beer getting shallow in the can. "Throw the sex in there, babe, don't forget the sex."

"Sex and Murder Self-Help book," I mused.

"That's it. You'd sell a million of 'em. I'd buy one. You want another brewski?"

"All right."

He waddled off to the fridge. "So how you think Marvelle got rich?" he called over his shoulder.

"Real estate. Drugs. Maybe her daddy is a chicken tycoon. What part of the South you think she's from?"

"Ozark twang," he said. "Arkansas maybe." He handed me a beer and heaved a sigh. "God, now my nuts really hurt."

I cracked my fresh beer and took a pull. On the top of the TV were two photographs, one a girl, the other a family portrait, both filmed with dust. I couldn't resist. I set my beer down and navigated the path to the television. The girl I picked up first, tilting the heart-framed photo in the dim light. Shelly watched me, slurping from his can. "Old girlfriend?" I said.

Shelly nodded. I put it down and took up the family photo. Shelly had not changed: same part in hair, same fallen lock over forehead, same ill-fitting brown corduroys, sleepy detached green eyes, and square chin. I'd never met his parents. His father was a beefy man, florid, with a navy haircut, a civil servant as I recalled, somewhere in his fifties in this picture, which had to be at least twenty years old. His mother was a small woman in a dress that looked like something a cardboard doll would wear. She wore a sun-squint expression, though the pose was indoors. Shelly used the term "airhead" more than any other to describe her. Standing next to Shelly was a swarthy young man with slicked back hair. He was a good six inches taller than Shelly, and with his cool and confident air didn't seem to fit in the picture. "Who's this?"

"My family."

"I mean the dark-haired kid."

"My brother, Donny Ray," said Shelly, stifling a yawn. "Donald Raymond Hubbard."

"Brother? I didn't know you had one."

"Yeah."

"Younger?"

"Four years."

"Same parents?"

He nodded drowsily. "Far as I know."

I looked back at the photo. "Looks like an athlete."

"Oh yeah, Donny did it all. Sax player, varsity football, swim team. Happiest kid I ever met. Got all the girls, too. Dad used to beat the tar out of me, but he'd never touch Donny Ray. My whole life I was convinced someone left him at our doorstep. Dad was always pretty nice to strangers."

"Where is Donny Ray?" I asked.

Shelly hauled back on his beer. "Dead."

I nodded, holding the picture, waiting for him to tell me the how and the when.

"How?" I said, finally.

"Dove off the Clam. Know it?"

"Yeah, of course." My head continued to nod as if the spring had come loose.

"Thirty-foot jump. Went face first into the rocks." He shrugged and looked away.

"How old was he?"

"Eighteen."

"You've never mentioned him before."

"It's not something I like to talk about."

"Jesus," I said. "I'm sorry."

He tipped his can back, draining it. "That's the kind of luck I've always had."

14. Jimmy Is In Good Hands With God

I WOKE LATE THE NEXT DAY AND STARTED A POT OF COFFEE. BEATRIZ had sewn me a pair of pajamas, blue tops, plaid orange bottoms, synthetic fabric that caused static electricity that felt like bugs crawling up and down my legs. I got her newspaper and fed Sweets, who'd told me he liked tortillas better than meat. Beatriz had driven up to Temple City to visit her daughter, so Sweets and I had the Island to ourselves. I thought I might take a long nap in the sun with him today. Sparrows were flitting among the splashes of sunshine in the orange tree in the central yard. The tree cast such a deep and realistic reflection in my front room window that the little birds would occasionally fly straight into the glass and fall stunned to the ground.

I opened the paper to look at jobs, then I leafed over to the sports. What a joy it was to recount the trip to Santa Anita and to see those payouts! If I moved up to L.A. I could probably make my living just standing at the rail and listening to the horses think. It was a notion that should've invigorated me, but I kept getting pictures of Shelly's brother, Donny Ray. I had dreamt of him all night, a tattered brown reel of cliff-diving dreams. In some of the dreams he was still alive, petitioning me, as if I could help him somehow. If he was four years younger than Shelly he would've been about my age. I was living in San Diego then, attending San Diego State University as a journalism major, and living off campus in an apartment on University Avenue. Journalism, which I was good at, was going to be my ticket to writing the great American horseracing novel. Times were good then, not a whiff of the pox that was soon to beset me. I tried to place Donny from the photograph or recall the story of a San Carlos boy diving off the Clam to his death, but there had been so many who had died on those rocks it was impossible to recount them all.

The pictures of Donny kept coming, beckoning to me. Finally, in the early afternoon, I put on my sunglasses, climbed into my pickup truck, and drove the few miles down the hill to La Jolla, home of the Clam.

La Jolla is an eccentric community, geographically and economically isolated, its own enclave. Even though it's part of San Diego, you have to write "La Jolla" on the envelope for it to get there. Many wealthy people live here, so I'm not much disposed to it, though in the days when I had out-of-town visitors, I was obliged to show them the Cove (site of numerous TV and movie scenes), and if they had a literary bent, take them on the Dead Writers Tour, starting with Raymond Chandler's home at 6005 Camino de la Costa and ending at Dr. Seuss's converted observation tower at the top of Mount Soledad. Both of San Diego's two famous writers lived and died in La Jolla but were born elsewhere. San Diego is not a literary wellspring. You're much more likely to run into a famous killer here. However, nowhere in its official annals is the city's most famous and prolific killer, so designated.

La Jolla is Spanish for "parking nightmare." I wandered around for about half an hour before I finally wedged into a tight spot at the bottom of the hill and walked up under the tall mottled palms. Down below the railed walkway, seals barked and yawped as the ocean waves clapped onto the rocky shore. One seal applauded, and I acknowledged it with a slight bow. An old woman bent from the weight of jewels dragged an ornamental rat of a dog at the end of its leash. A little tyke chased a flock of cormorants into a copse of stumpy cypress trees.

The Clam lies north of La Jolla Cove. Ask a lifeguard and he will pretend not to know where or what the Clam is. He doesn't want you to know. He doesn't want people jumping or diving off. He doesn't want to have to call the paramedics, doesn't want to have to scramble in himself and drag your broken bones up the smuggler's tunnel. He doesn't want helicopters flapping over, blood on his hands, nightmares, angry parents, journalists. He doesn't want to tell Mom and Dad that Donny is dead.

The notorious cliff was fenced off and NO DIVING signs were posted conspicuously, but it was public beach, legally accessible to all. Against the chain-link fence that symbolically prevented pedestrians from wandering down the treacherous bluff many memorials had been placed—rough crucifixes, baskets of flowers, ribbons, medallions, and crude reliquaries full of photos and postcards. Most salient among these was a large green handmade crucifix wired into the links. It had faded and roughened in the sea air, but the words written in black felt pen across the transverse piece were still clearly legible: JIMMY IS IN GOOD HANDS WITH GOD.

I walked around the fence and strolled down the limestone bluff, its gritty, eroding surface netted with tiny succulents. This promontory was so carved and worn by the endless action of wind and sea that in a few hundred years it would no longer exist. The diving arena was horseshoe- or clamshell-shaped, hence the name Clam. A lone palm stood to the left. The ocean smelled of kelp, fish, sea lion, iodine, and fermenting zooplankton. A yacht puttered far out to the south. A Channel Ten news team was close by to the north, divers jumping backward off the rocks.

I had always been afraid of high places not because I thought I might fall but because I thought I might jump, so it was with extreme reluctance that I moved into the area where Donny must have stood, where all divers must stand, and stared down dizzily into that grotto of sorrow thirty feet below. The shivering mosaic of blues and greens shifted against the coral. The exposed rocks were shiny round and black. The waves rolled in to cover them, then withdrew again.

No one, as far as I knew, had ever jumped with the intention of suicide here. Death would be too complicated, not a certain outcome by any means. The Cabrillo Bridge in Balboa Park (often called Suicide Bridge by the locals) and the Coronado Bridge over San Diego Bay were better, more effective choices for those who wanted to fly for a time before they died. So as shameful or grievous as Donny's death might've been to the family, I didn't imagine he had intentionally tried to end his life here. It had been all about the thrill, and perhaps the dare.

A diver's luck will depend on the tide. Thirty feet should be enough of a deterrent, but the jumper must also have good timing, must actually jump as the water has receded and is just returning. The entry point will almost always be shallow. A poorly timed jump or an improper entrance and you're feet or headfirst onto the rocks. And no number of signs or laconic lifeguards or horror stories can deter the young daredevils from taking their Acapulco chances. Prohibition, on the contrary, makes the risk all the more appealing. Every week in the paper San Diegans will read about some unfortunate child who's come here for the ecstasy of the dive only to bust his legs or crown. The last story I heard before moving north was two Vietnamese kids who made a successful jump but got caught in the surge and drowned. Nowhere did the signs read: "DANGEROUS CURRENTS."

To the north a hundred yards was the steep trail that led to the precipice called Dead Man's Jump, reputedly a hundred feet to the water. Just back from Dead Man's was a shell and gift shop. It'd been there longer than I could remember and was perched above a network of grottoes and caves, some of which had been used by bootleggers during Prohibition. One tunnel called the Sunny Jim Cave came straight up into the shell shop itself. This was the portal through which the injured and the dead were often transported. Bringing them up through the tunnel was easier than fishing them out with a helicopter or trying to drag them up the rocks with a rope. Public legend had it that the woman who ran the store had catalogued every poor soul who'd ever been carried up through her tunnel.

Lulled and drawn by the falling and retreating waves below, I finally tore myself away. Insidious chanting voices in my head, the palm tree to my left rattling like a snake, and hands out like a tightrope walker, I made my meticulous way back up the grade.

15.   Beauty Chasers

ONE NIGHT I HAD A DREAM THAT I HAD GONE TO SEE A MOVIE
called *Through the Looking Glass* that had been made in three Civil War
sequences and that I thought was going to be about Alice, who was four-
teen years old with slats of sunshine between her legs. But instead it turned
out to be someone's home movies on a lake. When I woke up the Sex and
Murder Self-Help Book had formed completely in my mind.

I had seen a typewriter through the window of cabin number 4.
One winter many years before, Charles Bukowski, the L.A. racetrack poet,
had rented cabin number 4 from my father to work. I was only a teen then
and opposed in principal to poetry, so he only seemed to me a pockmarked
crank who drank too much. My father did not like him either. Later, after
Bukowski got famous and my father and I were shown to be philistines, I
would admire him from a distance at any of the three southern California
tracks. There he'd be talking with a bartender, standing in a litter of los-
ing tickets, roaming with a plastic cup of whiskey, knit-capped, potbellied,
sometimes in high collar or black overcoat, leaning under the eaves blowing the steam off his coffee, the ever-present cigarette burning in his fingers. At Del Mar he stationed himself at the west end of the track by the
benches along the rail. He was always alone, the way he wanted it, the way
I and Shelly, who admired Bukowski for his father-tyrannized character
in *Ham on Rye*, kept it.

Now thanks to Beatriz I had the very manual Olympia, olive
green and solid as a tank, that he'd used to compose *South of No North* and
parts of *Factotum*. Off the meds, my fingers flew on the keyboard, just like
in the old days when I'd had to knock a column out in an hour. The writing

sailed along so smoothly I felt like a plagiarist or James Taylor composing "Fire and Rain." The keys struck faintly through the old ribbon just dark enough for a first draft. It could not hurt that the fingerprints of an uncompromising wino poet were somewhere under my own.

The thought of a self-help book fulfilled me. It was true self-help, especially if it could sell. I conceived it, as philosophy is divided, in five sections: beauty, ethics, logic, metaphysics, and epistemology, with a side trip into eschatology, the study of last things, like your Chinese wife walking away from you down Stinson beach hand in hand with the vice president of a watch company. Since most people who read self-help seek a substitute for religion, the emphasis would be on ethics. Within metaphysics I planned to discuss laughter, which for many of us takes the place of love. It was the best, anyway that I could do, and it was Shelly's ambergris, too, his miniature civilization rising above the merciless flood plains, plagues, and invasions of tragedy, his sweet smokestacks and hillbilly crushes and hilarious trees. What was it Kierkegaard said? The more one suffers, the more one has a sense for the comic. Love is no good either unless you've been through the wringer.

I should've been outlining, but found myself absorbed in the chapter on beauty. Beauty it seemed to me was the real flypaper of destruction. Beauty most of the time was an illusion, a deception, an invitation to a maelstrom. It was Sofia Fouquet believing that art would save her, or that lovely tropical island where I was hospitalized after being stung by six jellyfish. It was the alluring and duplicitous military strategist Alcibiades who "profaned the Eleusinian Mysteries" and eventually led his own Athenians to their downfall. It was sweet-scented Marvelle sitting on a blanket surrounded by rioting estrus-crazed orangutans.

Sweets slept at my feet, radiating remedial waves and cracking powerful eye-watering farts, his paws flipping in a chase dream. After a while he lifted his big sleepy head and said to me: *Shelly's coming up the drive.*

What's he doing here? I asked.

Not feeling well.

Sick?

Mother problems.

I got up and saw his truck through my window. "Shelly baby," I declared walking down the stairs to greet him. "How did you find me?"

"You told me where you lived."

"Fair enough. Come on in."

He followed me up the steps into my 1970s-themed cabin with its faded braided hippie rugs and four-pound black rotary telephone. "Who's the dog?"

"That's Sweets, the camp mutt. He won't bite. Everything all right?" I asked. "You don't look so good."

His head bobbled, his mouth turned down. "I'm okay."

"Keep thinking about that great day last week. Coffee?"

"Sure."

Taking the wing chair, he cast a wary glance at my typewriter in the kitchen. "You find a job yet?" he asked glumly. There was a hole in his shoe, I noted, as he dandled his foot up and down on his knee.

"Nah. Decided to write a bestseller instead."

"What bestseller?"

I filled the carafe and measured coffee. "Sex and Murder Self-Help."

"Oh, that." He nodded, knowing that I had no chance at success. A sparrow, seeing the reflection of the orange tree in my front window, flew with a sickening thump into the glass and dropped.

"Jesus," said Shelly, going to the window and peering down to examine the little fellow stunned on the grass below. "Poor bugger wasn't wearing his helmet."

"He'll be all right," I said. "They always hit claws first."

It disturbed me that I had shattered the ceiling lamp in my kitchen. I couldn't remember how or when it had happened. There was still some glass on the floor and I swept it up. Sweets stared at Shelly, his tail still.

Shelly was still looking out the window, his back to me, hands in pockets, when I approached with his mug. "Thanks," he said, wringing out a smile. He smelled faintly of bus depot and cheddar cheese.

I took a seat on the couch. The coffee scalded my mouth. Sweets came over and began to whisk his tail. "I'm writing a chapter on beauty," I said.

He sat down across from me. "Hmm."

"I've always wondered why people who chase after beauty end up jumping out the window or putting their head in the oven. Beauty's the opposite of happiness. I can count all the beautiful things that ever made me happy and fit them inside a Cheerio."

He nodded, distracted, blew on his mug. Whatever he drank, hot, sweet, cold, went down quickly in nervous gulps.

"You're a bit of a beauty chaser, it seems to me," I said.

He cracked a yellow grin. "I like sex if that's what you mean."

"I don't mean Bambi Woods or the whores in Tijuana, babe," I elaborated. "I mean your music. Your ideals. Coco Debbie. Your quixotic quest for God. Oh, and Marvelle, of course. You ready to go up this week and see her?"

He tried to laugh but coughed instead. "Can't," he said. His eyes began to shine then and he tried to blink it away. He massaged the bridge of his nose for a good thirty seconds before he spoke. "I didn't want to tell you this, but my mom is sick."

Sweets got up and trotted over to Shelly. Shelly patted him on the head. Sweets wagged his tail.

"Oh?" I said.

"Cancer," he said.

"What kind of cancer?"

"I don't know. It can't be too serious," he added quickly. "I don't think." He laughed, the incongruous laugh. "She won't die, that's for sure. All my family lives forever. They're like cockroaches." He spurt a puff of dry air, rolling his gaze about. "But I have to go back."

"To Alabama?"

He set his coffee in the window ledge. "Yeah."

He wanted to say something else, I saw, perhaps ask me a question, perhaps, "Will you come with me?" But he sealed his lips instead and stood.

"Well, I'd better go," he said. "Just wanted to let you know I won't be around for a while." He showed the broken forest of teeth, took a quick nervous gulp of empty mug and set it back down.

Shuffling to the door, he walked as if he'd been shot. I clapped his back. We never touched except for high fives. He was more solid than I recalled, downright heavy in the shoulders.

"I don't know when I'll be back," he said, with a doubtful glance over his shoulder.

I stood at the door. "Well, do what you need to do. I'll take care of the nags for you."

"I don't know what I'll do about my business. I've never left it longer than a week."

"It'll be all right. Japan can wait."

"Yeah," he said, and limped slowly down the deck stairs to his truck.

16.   Tales of Scottish Mastectomy

TWO WEEKS PASSED AND I COULDN'T STOP THINKING ABOUT
Shelly and his mother. One Tuesday I cruised by his house, Sweets the butterscotch brute perched on the passenger seat next to me. It didn't look as
if Shelly was home, and his truck was not in the driveway.

He in there, Sweets?

Don't think so.

How can you tell?

All that turmoil is pretty easy to pick up. He's as messed up as you.

You think so?

Birds of a feather.

What do you want to do?

*Let's go to the beach. I feel like frolicking in the waves. You don't
have a Frisbee, do you?*

I can pick one up. Need to get a Racing Form *and a couple of beers too.*

But the minute I pulled onto the freeway I was overcome with
pictures of Donny and messages I could not decipher.

Head full of static, I took the next exit, turned down the ramp,
felt suddenly prescient. And then I knew why. To the right was a Coco's. It
was *the* Coco's. It was also Tuesday, and I knew that there was a waitress
inside named Deborah who might be wondering where Shelly had gone,
and just once I decided I'd like to meet one of his mystery flames. Except
for some raw bok choy and the occasional handful of cashews, I had forgotten to eat for several days and my pants were sliding down my hips. I
pulled into the lot.

Hope you don't mind if I drop in here for a few minutes.

Sweets looked away.

It's Tuesday. I wonder if Shelly is in there.

He's in Alabama.

How do you know?

That's what you said.

You never know with Shell. It's not unusual for him to announce one thing when he intends another, just to clear himself some space.

Okay, so maybe he's in there. Bring me something to eat, a piece of fish or some French fries.

Coco's was slow, the limbo lull between lunch and dinner. My eyes scanned the restaurant for Shelly. There were a few oldsters killing time over coffee and a couple of even slower-moving young lovers in the corner, but no Shelly. I tried to imagine where Shelly would sit. That would depend, of course, on who Deborah was. There were three waitresses on duty, none I could rule out. I took a booth by the window.

Two ladies in the next booth over were having a discussion about mastectomy. The larger one, in a Scottish brogue loud enough for the whole restaurant to hear, bellowed: "On me way home from me first fittin' I've a new bosom there and I'm proud of it, but a *police* pulls me over, see. Well, I've put on muh seat belt—that was when they first passed the law, see—but he's starin' in at me like I've got three eyes. No one's ever looked at me quite like that before, Viv. I thought for a minute he fancied me. Well, he leaves me finally with a warnin' only. I was only five over the limit, see, and I think, well, I've blagged me way out of it. Only when he's gone do I look over and notice that me new tit is flung back over me shoulder!"

The ladies howled. The one named Viv appreciatively clanked her dish with a fork.

"Later that year I gets a newer model," she continued, "a bit more adherin', ye might say, and I'm out golfin' wi' me mucker, Emma, and I takes a mighty swing, and the whole business cooms flyin' out o' me blouse and lands out o' sight in the weeds. Well, Viv, we're down there lookin' about for the damn thing, see, and along come some old duffers to help. What are ye lookin' for? Well, says me mucker, she's lost her diddy. Oh, now shut up can ye a minute, Emma? I almost clubbed 'er, I did."

The ladies were screeching now, crying, slapping the table.

"It was that same year this weegie veterinary bloke I brings me dog to has this mutt and when I bend over to pet 'im he snatches away muh falsie, yanks it right out o' me brar and begins to shake it about. The bloody vet is in hysterics. It might be the fooniest thing he's ever seen. The man's a dobber, a bit of a boob 'imself, see? Gimme back me tit, ya daft beast, I says to him. I finally wrest it from him, but he's put teeth marks all in it, worse than me first 'usband. That was me third boob of the year, Viv. But I'll tell ye, only a month later, I'm in with me dog again, who snatches off the vet's hairpiece and scarpers off wi' it, shaking it about—ooh, well I never saw such a foony sight."

A waitress was standing above me, her notepad raised. She looked to be in her late thirties. She had haughty eyelids, pale irises. She was firm-jawed, straight-shouldered, masculine in bearing. Despite the amusing tales of Scottish mastectomy, her face was sad. Over the years I had come to appreciate sad people. The sad don't try to hustle you. They don't put on airs. Their feet are squarely on the ground. Sad people know the great secret of life, that it's not going to work out as you'd hoped. I noted there was no wedding ring. Her name tag read: RENEE.

"Good morning," Renee said. She had a subdued way of presenting herself. Subdued waitresses were rare in my experience. Her eyes were also subdued, perhaps Slavic eyes. I had had a Slavic girlfriend once who was very cruel to me and I still missed her.

She was also faintly familiar, but I could not place her. "Good morning," I returned.

"Are you ready to order?" she said.

I said, "Is there a waitress named Deborah employed here?"

Renee scrunched her brow. She wore bangs that shivered like Christmas tree tinsel. Her nose was not quite straight. She had that quick but lazy-tongued way of talking typical of southern Californians. "We had a Debbie, oh, I don't know, a year or so ago, but she only worked here for like three or four weeks. No one called her Deborah."

"You've been here a while."

"Two years." She blew upward out the side of her mouth and shivered the tinsel bangs.

"Two years is a long while."

She rolled her eyes. "Tell me about it."

"You didn't happen to go to Hoover High School?"

"How did you know that?"

"Lucky guess."

"Did you go to Hoover?"

"No, I went to Torrey Pines. We always said that Hoover sucked." Her bangs quivered. She studied me, tight lipped, trying to make a judgment about me. Her thoughts were bitter clear with the usual clutter of unspoken questions: Is he worth something or is he a crackpot? Is he giving or taking? Do high schools twenty miles apart in a big city truly count as common ground? And why does he look like a mangy penguin?

"Yes, I've heard all the Hoover jokes," she said. "We never won State because nature abhors a vacuum. It wasn't easy being a girl from Hoover."

"Well, you can console yourself with the fact that we never even had a stadium. We had to play all our games at San Dieguito."

She smiled at me, holding me in her sad gaze for a moment. Perhaps it was the sadness that seemed so familiar.

"I realize you're busy," I said. "I'll take the cod with coleslaw and fries. Coffee." I handed her the menu. "And a little bag for my dog."

She had a boyish backside that barely moved as she walked away. Maybe this was the girl that Shelly liked, right age, smart, unhappy, aloof, a more practical version of Marvelle, the kind of crush he could contemplate and make declarations about and encounter physically on a regular basis (kind of like a courtship) without obligation. He'd changed her name for storytelling purposes. Well, I had nothing but empathy for him. He wanted someone pleasant and compatible to share his life with and it wasn't going to happen. Sweets watched me intently from the truck window. The ladies behind me had paid their bill and were gone.

17.   Bee-doo Woman from Another Dimension, Possibly Hell

FOR WEEKS AS I RAN OUT OF MONEY AND HAD TO SUSPEND MY excursions to Foreign Book (the legal sports betting sites all over Mexico, now called Caliente Sportsbook) and my Tijuana cathouse forays and worked on my self-help book with Sweets healing my mind, I continued to hear nothing from Shelly. I thought he might call or write, just to give me an update or perhaps ask me to send along items he might've forgotten or that he couldn't get in Bay Minette, hot Mexican peanuts or a secondhand pair of corduroys or a can of 1958 California hair pomade. I was curious what the record market was like in the small-town South. Lots of Elvis, I imagined. Too bad they'd burned all that Beatles memorabilia after John's big flub about the Beatles being more popular than Jesus.

One day on Del Mar Heights I saw Shelly pulling out of an Arco station, no doubt, for the scorch marks up the side, it was Shelly's truck. I was about to turn around until I saw he had company, an awkward figure with a large head who, the stiff way it was leaned against the window, looked like a mannequin. Some people drove in the diamond lanes with dummies for passengers. Others I suppose were so lonely that their inflatable dates accompanied them wherever they went. I wondered why Shelly hadn't called or stopped by. The cab in which he sat crackled with dissonance, and it wasn't heavy metal or Stravinsky on the radio. I resisted the temptation to follow.

A couple of days later, still no word, I stopped by his house to check in on him. Sweets stayed in the truck. I didn't want him in a house where pets had been killed. It didn't feel right pulling that wooden knob at the end of the string that opened the clumsy latch on the other side of the gate. As I came down the walkway I heard muffled conversation, then a burst of music. To my right, the door that opened into the side of the garage was ajar. I peered in and saw the steel cage where his parents had imprisoned him for days at a time. Why would you keep the cage? I wondered. Why wouldn't you sell or give away the cage?

The dog next door was yapping frantically and throwing itself against the fence. I stood still for a moment, listening to Shelly's voice. "You said that Lily was your friend…"

The response was a muddle. The dog yapped and hurled itself into the fence, then yelped as its owner cursed and hauled it away.

Well, Shelly is home anyway, I thought. Burglars wouldn't be shouting and playing music. Shelly had a friend in there, I thought, a love interest, that was all, one of those special friends I never got to meet.

Still, he didn't have to let me in. My curiosity was strong. He was my only friend in the world and I just wanted to know about his mom and Alabama and if his business was okay. I'd leave him alone for another month if he wanted. I pulled back the screen and knocked lightly. I felt like Jem Finch standing at Boo Radley's door. I heard footfalls, the dropping of a chain, then the door squeaked open two inches and I was aware of one eye looking down at me like a madman from a castle tower. There was something about the large misshapen head that suggested Ronald Reagan. The door promptly closed.

Spooked, I turned and headed briskly for the gate. The argument resumed. Then the door opened a second time.

"Hey, Eddie." The voice of Shelly. The screen door creaked out. "I didn't know it was you. That goddamn dog…"

I turned, willing my heart to slow. "When you get back?" I said.

"Couple days ago."

I nodded. "Saw your truck parked out front."

"Yeah." He nodded along, as if he were warring with himself. "Hey, come in," he said.

"Just wondered how everything was going."

"Great," he said, laboring over a smile, his face a mask. "Haven't killed myself, anyway."

I stepped up through the door. The house was more decrepit than I recalled. I looked about for the partygoers, the arguers, the special friend. The TV was playing in the corner. The voice could have been Shelly's. He had a habit, like all of us loners, of talking to himself, very demonstratively sometimes, as if he were playing several different roles of Shelly and none too happy about any of them. If that was Shelly who opened the door the first time, then he most definitely had a multiple personality disorder. I decided that I wouldn't visit him again without advance notice.

I made out *I Love Lucy* on the box, closing credits. "So, well, uh," I ventured. "How's your mom?"

"Dead," he replied, picking up a *Racing Form* yellowing from age. He blinked at me and looked blindly at the *Form*. The way he was standing I could tell he was trying to block me off from a view down the hall. But I was ahead of him on this: I already knew there was someone down that hall and I had no desire to see them.

"I'm sorry," I said. "That was fast."

"You want a beer?"

"All right."

He shuffled into the kitchen, stooped as an old man, and retrieved two beers. That open slot on the couch hadn't filled yet so I dropped into it, glancing over at Dick Van Dyke pratfall BWAP-BOP. I noted that the cushion underneath me was warm.

Shelly poised at the edge of the chair at his business table opened his beer in a trance. His voice had a faraway quality, as if he were channeling from another dimension. "She was almost gone when I got there," he said. "Went up into her brain. Never knew she had one. I mean brain cancer was the one thing I was never worried about." He chuckled, a sound more like sobbing. "My father, that asshole." His voice drifted off for a moment. He stared at his beer that he hadn't yet touched. "I thought it would be good when she died. Justice. Like the Nuremberg Trials." He wagged his head for a while, eyebrows converged. "But she was like Adolf Eichmann, you know, just taking orders."

Swinging his head, he seemed to be thinking long back. He hadn't touched the beer. "Still, she could've stopped him, said something. Could've come late at night with a glass of water. They never even let me have water." He choked as if his throat were dry, then looked about helplessly, not seeing me. He hadn't shaved for a while. His beard was sparse, his eyes puffy and red. He was a grieving middle-aged adult in brown cords, plaid shirt, and dull brown clodhoppers, but I swore he looked five. The television burned its ancient cheery childhood scripts. For the second time in four minutes Dick Van Dyke fell on his ass.

I said nothing, not even sure he was aware I was in the room.

"I feel no relief," he said, his voice pinched with anguish.

I nodded.

"I wanted to tell her something before she died."

"What did you want to tell her?" I said gently.

His face contorted in confusion, he twisted his head around so that he was staring into the kitchen with one eye, the eyebrow above it tangled as old wire. "I wanted to tell her to go to hell." He cracked a mean yellow grin. "But I figured she was going there anyway."

"Do you think Eichmann went to hell?"

He shrugged, disinterested in the fate of the infamous Nazi war criminal.

"Anyway," I said. "You don't believe in hell."

"Oh, I believe in hell all right," he said, spreading his arms. "I've seen it, man." He roared with laughter and finally took a healthy slug from his can. "I tell you about this woman that came along, came out of nowhere and started taking care of my mom?"

"No."

"She had this hairdo like the Leaning Tower of Pisa, and she wore these white bellbottoms and a lime-green plaid blouse. I thought she worked for the hospital, but she didn't. Then I thought she was a friend of the family or a neighbor. She wasn't. Then I thought she might be a ghoul, but what kind of ghoul comes to a hospital and helps an old lady dying of cancer? She kept smiling at me like she knew."

"Knew what?"

"I don't know."

"Maybe she was an angel."

"I don't know why it wasn't him that died."

Now I heard talking again, down the hall.

Shelly didn't seem to hear it. My beer was gone. I was the nervous drinker now. Shelly stared wearily through me. He'd lost at least ten pounds. Now something broke down the hall, followed by a cry.

Shelly set his teeth, whispered "Jesus," set down his beer, rose, and marched away. I heard a "Shut up, will you? I've got company. Just sit down." A radio clicked on, the song "Venus," by Shocking Blue. "Play with this."

He returned, shaking his head and offering no explanation. "Keep thinking about that woman with the bee-doo hair," he resumed, hands on hips. "You know what she was?" He stared at me intently, the first time I'd felt as if I existed in the room.

I flicked up my shoulder.

"My real mom. The mom I should've had." He wiped his mouth with the palm of his hand. "I even thought about, you know, going with her, but then again maybe she was from down there. Had to show Mom the way. Because the minute my mother died, and that lady was right there holding her hand, well she was gone. I looked for her too." He scratched his head, hauled from his beer, finishing half the can in one tilt.

"You want to get out of here?" I asked. "Go someplace and get a couple of beers?"

He looked up, considering the offer. He might've aged two years. He was honestly perplexed by the woman with the bee-doo hair. "No, man, I gotta get my business back up. I've got about a hundred orders I need to fill. Couple of pissed off people called." He glanced down the hall. "Lucky I don't speak Japanese."

"How about Santa Anita on Sunday?" I suggested.

"Hell," he said, his barrel chest heaving with a sigh. "I've even lost track of the nags."

"We can drop in on Marvelle."

His eyes glinted for a moment, but then whether it was his mother or his guest or the thought of being obliged to a flesh-and-blood Marvelle, the light in his eyes subsided.

"I'll give you a call," I said.

"Yeah, all right," he said, already raising his right hand to close the door behind me.

18.   Martha at the Apollo

ANOTHER WEEK PASSED BEFORE I HEARD FROM SHELLY AGAIN. HE called me on the phone. I thought he'd finally caught up on bookwork and was a go for live racing at Santa Anita and a little sidetrip to see a Girl in a Heart-Splashed Blouse. I was ready for him to say, "Let's hit the track, babe."

He said instead, plainly distressed, "Can you come over?"

"Now?"

"Yeah, if you can. I'm in kind of a bind."

I jumped into my truck and drove the thirty miles inland, six miles an hour over the speed limit. Both the gate and the front door were open when I arrived. Shelly was standing in the living room, waiting for me, hands clasped in front of him.

"My father is sick now," he said. "The same cancer as my mother."

"Wow," I said.

"I've got to go back again. Can you watch my business for me?"

"Your business."

"Yeah. I can't let it fall apart again. I'll go under."

"I don't know anything about it, babe."

"Who sang 'Jimmy Mack'?"

"Martha and the Vandellas."

"See?"

"Yeah, but I don't know what label. I don't know the prices. I don't know what gown she wore at her debut at the Apollo."

"You know your music, babe," he said. "Anyway, I got no one else I can trust. You got a job yet?"

"No," I said, my sexy self-help book composed on a celebrity typewriter having gone into a stall.

"I'll make it worth your while. I can't lose my biz. All you gotta do is fill orders, pick up my mail at the P.O. No phone answering. No hustling. No more than two hours a day. I'll give you fifty bucks a day, plus 10 percent commission on all sales. I'll be back in two weeks, a month tops. I don't think he'll die, anyway."

My ears had begun to sweat. "I guess I could."

"Can you stay here, too?" he asked. "There have been some break-ins in the neighborhood recently, and I've got some valuable records. You can sleep wherever you like and use my typewriter if you want."

I had a good look around and repeated the feeble phrase. "I guess I could."

"I've got to leave tonight. Let me show you around. The place is yours. Listen to any records you like."

19.   Psychotic Reaction

BY THE TIME I RETURNED WITH A FEW OF MY THINGS TO SHELLY'S
house that evening, Shelly was gone. The sun had turned red over the
housetops. Shelly planned to drive straight through, with only rest-stop
naps and hamburgers, as he had the last time. He did not like motels. He
had no insurance, so he was a night driver, a self-proclaimed rabbit killer.
He followed the back roads, the secondary highways. He'd looked so lost
when I had shaken his hand and wished him a good trip, but he'd also been
open and hospitable in a way that I'd never seen. I doubt that few had seen
this side of him. He didn't really need or believe he needed other people. I
didn't imagine that, outside of Mexican dentists, he'd ever had to rely on
anyone as much as he was about to rely on me.

    As a rule, I don't like horror movies because their success is
predicated on a protagonist who insists on going where good sense tells
him he should not. On a bet long ago I slept in a mountain cabin in Cuyama-
ca, where a camper had been murdered and where his spirit supposedly still
resided. There was also the additional danger of the murderer, still at large.
I can't say I slept. And though I won the bet, it was also the first time I expe-
rienced a psychotic episode, unless I really did see a full apparition of the
murdered camper and a man with a hatchet in the window.

    Now another haunted cabin, another bet. This one had much
more riding on it: my promise, a man's business, perhaps a man's sanity, perhaps my sanity. I picked up the checklist he'd written for me and
reviewed it once again.

1.   Check post office box daily.
2.   Wait till check clears on new clients before filling orders.

3. All records are alphabetical by ARTIST.
4. Make sure conditions of records are accurate.
5. For record prices use Giddings.
6. Petty Cash in band-aid box in medicine cabinet.
7. Extra house key in magnetic box in back of mailbox.
8. Don't throw away paper trash, receipts, addresses, can't let people find that, just bag it and I will burn it when I return.
9. Good luck.

List in hand, I wandered once again through the maze of Shelly's afflicted sanctuary. I kept getting this feeling that I wasn't alone. My imagination would not allow me to believe that the special friend had left the house. Compulsively, restively, I checked again each room. His parents' bedroom was a dusty mausoleum with heavy peach-colored Queen Anne drapes and the reek of mothballs. On the walls were several staid and yellowed world-conqueror portraits: Hannibal, Tamerlane, Akbar the Great, Hitler, and Alexander the Great, who raped his way all the way to India and therefore could not have been that Great. Shelly's disheveled bedroom was so cluttered with *Racing Forms*, clothes, and memorabilia that there was barely a navigable path to the unmade bed. Donny's room, cool and sterile as the ghost it represented, was, Shelly had told me, unchanged since his death.

It was the stale chill air in this house, I decided, the palpably undisturbed layers of sorrow and neglect, that unnerved me. Pain is a noumenal stain that soaks into walls and fixes itself like a scent in the air. Pain, like smell and flavor, is a form of memory. You can feel the warmth of a loving house and in places like psychiatric hospitals and halfway houses and The Hubbard Museum of Pain you can feel its inimical opposite. I was tempted to hire a priest or a shaman, perhaps leave an open Bible in the middle of each room and come back next week. I wanted to clean the place up, open the curtains at least, let in some air and light. Have a chat with the spirits. Listen, I'm just here to look after Shelly's business. I have no interest otherwise. It wasn't my idea to stay here.

I turned the TV on, as Shelly would've done, to mask the silence. *The Adventures of Ozzie and Harriet* flickered up, one of the blandest most soporific sitcoms ever made. But Shelly worshiped this show and could recite entire episodes by heart. He didn't view this series as entertainment but as a training manual or a family documentary, an electronic how-to manual on the reconstruction of a shattered past, but how could this do anything, I wondered, since the Nelson family portrayal wasn't remotely real, except widen the gulf between himself and his unattainable ideals?

I moved all the items I'd brought—blanket, pillow, flashlight—to the record room, the only sane room in the house, a converted bedroom with painted wooden shelves on every wall to the ceiling. Each square cubby hole was filled with a neat leaning stack of sleeved vinyl. Shelly had several cubbies marked NO SALE. He made most of his money selling junk to Asians and Europeans. The good stuff he kept for himself. I rummaged through them: a Beatles' Butcher Block (the original controversial cover of *Yesterday and Today*, with the lads posing draped with meat and dismembered naked dolls, was recalled and then pasted over with a more congenial cover and re-released; but you could tear away the second cover and, if you were lucky, find yourself a rare Beatles collectible underneath); a ten-and-a-half-inch Stowaways on Justice Records; a Johnny & the Jammers (Johnny Winter); the Infatuators on Fellatio Records; a promo copy of "In the Hands of Karma" by the Electric Toilet; a sample copy of "Ring Chimes" by the Dots; a stereo version of "Bring Down the House" by the Escorts; a blue vinyl copy of a Five Satins single; and the crown jewel of his collection, Jackie Brenston's "Rocket 88" on Chess Records with Ike Turner on guitar, asserted by many to be the first rock and roll record ever issued. (The record was a 1954 reissue delta-marked, 1954, but no original 1951 recordings, according to the pricing guides, were known to exist.)

As a child I collected coins. It was exciting to dream that one day I might find in circulation a coin that would make me rich. But I never found anything worth much more than eight bucks. Too many people hoarded old coins. It you wanted a truly valuable coin you had to go to a dealer and pay what it was worth, hope for market appreciation and in the interim the joy of ownership. But coins are dull. They don't sing songs. They contain no emotion, risk, love, no passion, art, memory, little history, and nothing human beyond the oil and dirt from spenders' pockets and hands. Even if Shelly never made a plug nickel for all his effort, I marveled at what a cultural gold mine he'd amassed.

I was about ready to set "Rocket 88" on the turntable to hear it for the first time when the phone rang, startling me. No chance I would answer. Shelly would only be a city or two down the road. I glanced at my watch. Four rings and a stop. I wandered back down the hall, into the living room, and unplugged the phone from the wall, feeling guilty and wondering where Jackie Brenston was. Shelly's guide told me that his Delta Cats weren't even assembled at the time of the recording, and that Ike Turner composed the song, and what could that have been like, composing the first rock and roll song ever? Ike Turner would nevertheless be remembered for the rest of his life as the beater of his ex-wife Tina.

I checked the fridge to find nothing but shreds of cardboard from torn-open twelve packs and a few portion-control packets of Jack-in-the-Box hot sauce. The freezer was blocked with speckled ice. There was a sound down the hall, a sort of furry thump. I'd already explored every room, high and low, bed, closet, tub. Possibly I'd left the record player on, and the arm had kicked back on its own.

I told myself there was no one here. The intruders, the phantoms, were in my mind. The threats, as they were in the mountain cabin, and as I walked the streets of San Jose stealing suits and insulting strange women, were figments, residual at best, a torment that didn't possess the substance to physically reach me. I had to get a grip. Still, I couldn't sit or relax. I turned off the television. I didn't want to play music anymore for fear I might be unable to hear the sound again. I returned to Donny's room, the origin it seemed to me of the disturbance, and of all the noises before. I noted that the bedspread was rumpled as if someone had recently slept here. This is where the secret friend resides, I realized, though I couldn't conceive of sleeping in what amounted to a dead boy's altar. Again I checked the closet and looked under the bed. I promised myself I would not dwell in this room. It was, as Shelly described, a Donny Ray shrine. On the walls were San Diego Padres banners, Alice Cooper posters, a framed high school diploma, the lyrics of a Chicago song, "Colour My World," written in felt pen in a feminine hand. There was a bottle of Hai Karate on the dresser along with a desiccated corsage, ticket stubs, and a religious trinket. Beads hung from the neck of a bust of Jim Morrison. Above the bed was a large portrait of the same girl who resided on Shelly's TV set. I had asked Shelly if that was a girlfriend. It was apparently a girlfriend, just not Shelly's. I opened a photo album and studied the many pictures of the same girl. She was leaned down, hands on knees, mouth open. She was diving for a volleyball. Here she was in a bikini, looking very trim. I sat down on the bed.

On a table to the left was a reel-to-reel player, a black Marantz model, state of the art in its day, a tape threaded in. Below the player in a milk crate were boxes of tapes. One was marked "Donny's favorite songs, 1986."

Nineteen eighty-six? He would've been many years gone.

I pushed the button on the reel-to-reel to hear the song "Venus" by Shocking Blue. I rewound about ten minutes' worth and pressed play. The voices were from a distance. One was Shelly's. The other was unintelligible. Shelly was upset: "I took the brunt of Dad's shit. You went to the beach. I don't care if you don't remember. You said that Lily was your friend—well, I never felt that way…" A dog was yapping throughout. "Goddamnit, I told you not to answer the door." There was a pause, the sound of footsteps, the sound of harsh breathing, then my voice, the front door closing, a conversation about Adolf Eichmann. I'd never liked the sound of my voice. Someone was standing by the player it sounded like, breathing in a careful but labored way. A crash, even though I knew it was coming, made me jump. The thump of footsteps up the hall again: "Shut up, will you? I've got company. Just sit down." The radio clicked on, the song "Venus" by Shocking Blue. "Play with this."

I snapped off the player and headed for the front door.

20.   The Missing Prostitutes

I COULDN'T LET SHELLY DOWN OR PERMIT HIS BUSINESS TO GO
under or allow someone to break into his Cracker Jack box of a house and
steal his "Rocket 88" or Electric Toilet or "Ring Chimes" by the Dots, and
his house was the perfect hideout since I had talked to my father who said
a detective asking about me had stopped by and I didn't know how long
I could trust him before he spilled the beans. So I went back to the Island
and got Sweets and a King James Bible and a bottle of Presidente brandy. I
apologized to Sweets about the killing of pets. Sweets pointed out that forgiveness, along with gratitude, spontaneity, and eating stale food without
complaint, was his bag. He had a good sniffing all around and confirmed
that no one was there.

    So, what I am I receiving? I wanted to know.

    Fear, he said. *Crimes.*

    What kind of crimes?

    All kinds, he replied.

    Killing?

    Yes.

    People, I mean.

    Yes.

    Old or new?

    Both.

    Men or women?

    Hasn't been a woman in this house for years.

    I took a slug from my brandy and let it glow in my gullet. *Is
Shelly a killer, Sweets?*

Someone *in this house is.*

Man, am I a magnet for killers, I said.

That's because you're corrupt, came the reply.

All humans are corrupt.

Not to your degree.

Well, I'm working on it.

I hope you brought tortillas.

Forgot, sorry. How about a can of tuna?

Tuna will be fine.

21.   The Bones of *La Zona Basura*

THE DAYS PASSED PLEASANTLY ENOUGH IN THE COMPANY OF Sweets. We listened to records. We sat out in the yard, feeding peanuts to the blue jays (as Shelly was fond of doing). We cuddled and took naps. On Saturday nights we had pork chops and popcorn and watched a movie together. Now and then I'd dredge up one of Sofia's made-up camp songs ("Faaar From the Outhouse on a Cold and Runny Night" was Sweets's favorite) and get him to sing, which he did with gusto. I thought of Sofia often and ran memories of her like magic lantern slides through my head, revisiting the time we'd organized the first (and last) Wienerschnitzel Parade, and the day she and I had taken on Morris and his Tagalog social worker buddy, Angelo, in a game of two-on-two basketball. She was an ace from the three-point line, and though I couldn't shoot for beans I was four inches taller than Morris, gleefully boxing him out for every board and assuring our five-dollar victory: 21–3.

I studied the Giddings, memorized collectibles, read up on bands and songs. I closed off all the parts of the house I didn't need, sealing Donny's bedroom with a hook that latched curiously from the outside. I rolled sheet after sheet into the platen of my typewriter, staring into the white wilderness of what was supposed to be the chapter on ethics. I mowed the lawn and pruned back that thornapple tree whose branches were growing into the neighbor's yard. Shoring the fence with a piece of angle iron where the dog hurled itself every time he heard me coming through the gate, I knocked it down to reveal a woman and her daughter sunning topless. The mother said, "What are you looking at, asshole?" Sweets made a run at the yapper, who was lucky to get back through his little pet door in time. The neighbors cursed me once more and I fixed the fence so that it would not fall again.

As my Sex and Murder Self-Help continued to fizzle, a deep and complicated melancholia began to seep into my soul. Fat people when they become thin realize that only the misery that made them fat in the first place is there to welcome them, as is often the case with the long-incarcerated released to a stigmatized life without purpose, structure, or companionship: a life in which freedom is a burden. I fell back into old mental health strategies: comparing myself to those worse off than I, attempting to live in the moment, reminding myself of God's mercy and His plan. I recited New Age saws: everything has a reason; be grateful for the simple things. When those failed, I switched to heavy but equally useless doses of darker wisdom: life is tragic, no one gets out alive; pleasure is transitory, existence is an illusion. I had known people, like Flightless, who'd been spared from their date with death, and who'd done nothing with their extra days except make things worse for themselves, as if not dying at their appointed time had been a karmic violation. I wondered if Napa State Hospital had been my fate, if I had died with Sofia (as I'd wanted), and I was now only a ghost whose greatest power was scavenging vinyl and annoying my topless neighbors. Aware that somehow I needed to forget myself, for the first time in my life I fell back on my father's method for killing the days without killing myself: I worked.

Shelly's catalogues, his guides, his pricing, were all in need of an update. His Xeroxed order forms were fading. His accounting system was in disarray. He needed to expand the catalogues. Why, if the Japanese liked Ed Ames and Dinah Shore, wouldn't they want Eydie Gormé and Paul Anka too? There was no inventory for some of the orders, so I had to go through other dealers in a less profitable arrangement to find the requested records. Shelly needed to put everything up on a computer and save himself a few hundred hours of work. I didn't know how many dealers had international mailing lists and were exploiting the vinyl Pat Boone market in Norway, but eventually the internet would supplant his post-office-box-and-money-order business. Unfortunately, Shelly was a Luddite who enjoyed exclaiming that he "didn't even know how to turn a computer on," (there's a switch right on the front there, babe, I'd tell him), and so for all the time I knew him he was committed solely and stubbornly to the old-fashioned mail-order-catalogue method.

One day, looking for stamps in Shelly's desk, I came across a scrapbook full of news clippings about the butchers, torturers, cannibals, and vampires he so esteemed. He'd been keeping this book since the 1960s, starting with the Zodiac Killer, who'd never been caught. The bulk of the book was dedicated to local killers, no shortage of those. There were several articles about the Green River Killer, who many thought had migrated from Washington State to operate in the wooded areas of east and north San Diego. Then there was Cleophus Prince, Jr., dubbed the Clairemont Killer, a black mother-haunted chap who stabbed his white female victims with repeated frenzy in their chests. The Marine serial killer Andrew Urdiales had started killing prostitutes in his home state of Illinois before his pathological talents were relocated to Camp Pendleton and consequently the unfortunate prostitutes of San Diego. Ramon Rogers was a TV actor and a heavy metal drummer who managed an apartment building in east San Diego and dismembered his close friends with a jigsaw and bolt cutters. Shelly lived in San Carlos, so he had also enshrined the San Carlos Triumvirate: David Allen Lucas, an awkward bullet-headed kid who had cut the throats of many women and children; sixteen-year-old Brenda Spencer, who'd shot students of Grover Cleveland Elementary School (the same school Shelly had attended) across the street from the window of her home because she claimed to not like Mondays, yielding a hit single for the Boomtown Rats called "I Don't Like Mondays"; and Eagle Scout Daniel Alstadt, who after being prohibited from attending a keg party by his authoritarian father, chopped up his entire family—father, mother, sister, brother, and dog—with a hatchet, started his San Carlos home on fire, and went to the party. Lucas was on death row at San Quentin. Spencer, whose school shooting had kicked off a national trend, continued to be refused parole. Alstadt hanged himself in his cell. All three of these killers had struck within the same decade and the same square mile. Murder was definitely in the air in Shelly's quaint suburban neighborhood.

In another section of this scrapbook, toward the back, were several backpage briefs about missing Tijuana prostitutes. I wondered why Shelly would clip, much less save them. I could determine no dates, though by the newsprint I could tell they were fairly recent. No bodies had been found, no doubt due to the usual public apathy surrounding ladies of the night, but in one of the longer stories, the only one with a hook, it was mentioned that human bones had been recovered from the great incinerator at *La Zona Basura*, Tijuana's largest landfill. And though no forensic connection between the burned bones and the vanished hookers had been made, there was prevailing suspicion in the mind of the Tijuana chief of police that the bones belonged to the missing prostitutes.

I returned the scrapbook to its drawer and began to wonder again about Shelly's claim of multiple personalities, his fractured but carefully partitioned life, his instability, long suffering estrangement, frustration with women, necrophilic fantasies, his long disappearances, his absence of official identity, his frequent expeditions into Tijuana to "straighten out the mess in his head," and those scorch marks up the passenger's side door of all his pickup trucks.

22.   Mo Ho

MY GROWING INABILITY TO WATCH TELEVISION FOR FEAR THAT IT was stealing my thoughts, brief periods of amnesia and lost time, that fellow approaching in the black overcoat with impulse camera lenses for eyes, the notion that I might somehow be on the verge of isolating the "spice" of the eighth sense, a daylong Tijuana infatuation with obtaining a nonexistent tequila called Monstruo that possessed occult powers, my coffee crystal revelations that had no bearing on the subjects I was attempting to address, my tendency toward echolalia and word transposition, my active fantasy that I was being interviewed by a late-night talk show host, and my rising rage when I encountered a female stranger, were all warnings I should've heeded.

But I told myself that a few bumps and blowouts and stormy days down any highway were to be expected. I surely wasn't going to call Jangler over a handful of minor episodes. And though every schizophrenic I had ever known had been capable of only destructive plots, my view had been tainted by being housed with chronically criminal psychotics. Many more others like me sat harmlessly in wicker chairs playing bridge in sunny sanitariums. Still others functioned benignly and contributed to society. There were even examples of stark-ravers who flourished despite (or perhaps even because) of their affliction: John Nash, who won the Nobel Prize in economics; the artist Louis Wain and his electric Hindu cats; dozens of musicians, including space-rocker Syd Barrett, a founder of Pink Floyd, and blues great Peter Green from Fleetwood Mac; and myriad other Poes, Goyas, El Grecos, and van Goghs.

Neither did I intend to return to medication. My dyskinesia was down to faint tremors. Any possibility of spontaneous recovery, slim as it was, got slimmer under the influence of neurologically toxic antipsychotics, which I now understood were designed to be addictive and therefore to supply an endless river of revenue into the reservoirs of the pharmaceutical companies. The classic psychiatric description of psychosis is an individual untethered from reality, but it seemed more precise to say that this same individual had gotten untethered somehow from the *truth*. And the truth was not drugs, so I vowed, as Jangler had advised from the beginning, to commit myself to clarity and lucidity whenever possible, to resist temptation, murmurous superstitions, and chimerical talk show hosts, to stop dividing myself against what I could not naturally achieve. As my own life improved I would endeavor to improve the lives of others, not just by putting coins in charity cans and recycling my aluminum but by being a good neighbor, paying the utmost attention to the operation of Shelly's business, deferring to the instincts of my long-neglected soul, and reinvigorating my stalled self-help book by moving it out of the genre of vulturous pop quackery into a less profitable but hopefully more utilitarian category of observations based on personal experience. I intended to call it *Benevolent Madness: A Manual for Recovering Schizophrenics.*

Fifty percent of Shelly's mail was from Japan. About 30 percent came from Scandinavia. Looking back, I marvel at how Shelly ran his business with faded Xeroxed catalogues, checks, and money orders, all of it conducted at a snail's pace through the narrow slot of a P.O. Box, an unthinkable and completely impractical arrangement for a dealer of Shelly's ilk today. One of Shelly's devoted customers, a bar owner in Barcelona, was obsessed with Don Ho. The French wanted jazz (*je regrette*). The Swedes loved surf music, and with all that ABBA right up to their eyebrows, I knew they'd love punk, but Shelly didn't deal in punk. Punk was smut to him. So were rap, heavy metal, and disco. He had a few discriminating customers, that fellow in the Hague, for example, who couldn't get enough Cannonball Adderley. There was the occasional letter in English, but the majority of the order forms were simply accompanied by money orders, personal checks, and the occasional international reply coupon or envelope of U.S. cash.

These orders were not hard to fill. Shelly shipped his vinyl discs, bubble-wrapped and cardboard slip-covered, in flat boxes. Most people ordered multiple records because the shipping price of five records was only nominally more than the cost of shipping one. The Japanese, who loved fifties and sixties Americana more than Americans did, would take almost anything from that period, especially if the singers had been TV or movie stars like Ricky Nelson, Jim Nabors, Dean Martin, or Dinah Shore.

I opened three to six envelopes a day. The postal clerks, all three of them, were delighted to hear that I represented Shelly Hubbard. I was treated as if I were royalty. "Hey, so where is the old fuss budget?"

"He had to go back to Alabama," I explained.

"His mom?"

"Dad this time."

"Oh no." Their faces registered genuine concern. This was my first experience with post office emotion. I was impressed but not surprised by the scope of Shelly's charm. The clerks stressed to me that whatever it was I might need that I should please let them know.

Week two watching Shelly's business, I got a postcard from him:

Doctors say Dad will die soon, but they don't know him. The track here is no good, even if they run all year. All the horses are lame. Birmingham's not a llamadrome but a lame-o-drome. It's like *Return of the Mummy*. I can't play thousand-dollar claimers. How goes it with you?

By the end of the second week I'd run out of Don Ho. The Barcelona bar owner had made a run on me and his customers still wanted mo' Ho. Shelly never said anything about replenishing stock, but he did say if I needed anything, petty cash was in the medicine cabinet. There was over four hundred dollars stuffed into the Band-Aid box, and since I was getting a 10 percent commission on all sales I didn't mind funding some of the effort out of my own pocket.

Don Ho won't be hard to find, I thought. In my mind was a picture of a thousand garage sales and in each a box full of Don Ho, but as I flipped through the garage-sale boxes I found no amiable Hawaiian faces. I saw a lot of Christmas albums, *Chicago XVIII* through *XXI*, Mantovani, *One Hundred & One Strings Orchestra*, the balladic efforts of an actor who played in a popular police drama, endless hairy dope children, polka players, dancing polyester schlockmeisters, cowboy crooners, blues stealers, and vacant clean-cut Dylan clones with Brylcreemed heads and big wooden guitars.

On Sunday I hit the swap meet at the Aero Drive-in in El Cajon and struck out there, too, though I loaded up on Elvis, Bobby, Ricky, Pat,

Debbie, Dinah, and Doris. The Japanese, unlike their counterpart Scandinavians, worshiped blonds, even those who couldn't sing. And no one was going to argue that this Loggins and Messina album was worth any more than seventy-five cents. Nevertheless, there were Portuguese teenagers who would pay seventeen dollars for a copy of *Mother Lode*, not including shipping, without batting an eye.

Which didn't address the Don Ho desires of the Barcelona saloonkeeper, so on Monday I ventured to one of Shelly's regular dealers, a used record store in Del Mar. I was over my head here. There were no bargains, no steals, no exploiting market differentials. The records were pricey, more the realm of coin collecting, where you could get what you wanted but had to pay the going rate. I wouldn't net for Shelly or myself any kind of reasonable profit. And Don Ho should have been a 700 percent prospect, minimum. Nevertheless, I needed that Ho.

One of the clerks recognized me. "Hey, you're Shelly's buddy, right?

"That's me. Willie Wihooley." I put out my hand.

He nearly embraced me. "I'm Dirk," he said. "Where's the kid?"

"Had to go back to Alabama." I gestured east with my thumb.

Dirk nodded for a while. "You don't say?"

"I'm sort of running his business for him. His mother died and now his father is sick."

"I heard about his mom." He bit his lip. "Gee, that's tough."

"Yeah."

"Well, I got the best prices for you, man." He clapped my shoulder. "You just tell me what you're looking for. Everything's 50 percent off for you."

"Hey, thanks." I felt as if I'd been swept into a secret society. Everywhere I went in Shelly's World the mention of his name rolled out the red carpet. I drifted back toward standards, and found Mr. Ho not far from his antithesis: Billie Holiday. There were five Ho albums in stock. I scooped them all hoping I hadn't blown the cover on Shelly's secret international treasure-trash niche. At three bucks each against international market price I could still turn 600 percent profit. Fish in a barrel. Why were there not a thousand people doing what Shelly was doing?

As I turned away from the register, Dirk called after me. "Well,

Willie, you tell Old Shell we miss him. I got some Crystals and a 1910 Fruit-gum Company I've been holding for him."

They all think he's wonderful, I thought. Shelly was smiling somewhere, I could almost see him, and I wondered as the door jingled closed on my heels if he could see me.

23.   Whirlaway

AT SIX EVERY MORNING I WAS OUT THE DOOR. SHELLY'D ASKED ME for only two hours a day, but I found record hunting an exciting, profitable, and purposeful pastime. With all its puzzles, mazes, codes, and footnotes, its scholarly requisites, and its suitability to the solitary life, the game of record hunting resembled in many ways the sport of kings. It helped to know where and what to look for, but anyone with enough luck and persistence might catch a winner, a Five Satins on blue vinyl, a copy of "They Say," by Herbert Milburn and the LeSabres on Zebra Records, a Robert Johnson, or a "Rocket 88." I'd recently read about "Whirlaway," the 45-rpm turntable that played something called the "Whirl-Away Demonstration Record" named after the famous racehorse who won the Triple Crown in 1941. "Only two copies of the record," my guide stated, "probably the first 45 ever made expressly for promotional purposes, are known to exist today, though others likely survive."

I'd developed my own circuit by now and each day a better understanding of where to find what I needed. Besides the armloads of profitable chaff I harvested daily, I had hit three minor jackpots, "See" by Jan and Dean on Dore, 1960, worth about a hundred bucks, Larry Donn's (with the Killer Possum Band), "Girl Next Door," (even if it was scratched, it played and was worth about seventy-five dollars), and Fats Domino "Goin' Home" on Imperial, near-mint condition, worth about three hundred.

Like Shelly, I got less satisfaction out of making 800 percent off a Tijuana Brass album than I did finding a legit classic or collectible. You'd never guess how many groups there were, how many "made it" but were never heard from again; or had a small or regional hit soon forgotten; or who had genius or success written all over them but chickened out, turned to drugs, blew the contract, couldn't get along; or someone in the group died or went mad; or they were mismanaged; or they got discouraged at poor sales and disbanded only to see success and get back together after the magic was gone. You might know the forlornly, fantastically sublime tune "Sunny," which Bobby Hebb wrote after his brother was killed in a knife fight the day after JFK was assassinated, and he's actually trying to sing it upbeat.

On the fourth Monday picking up Shelly's mail there was a postcard from him that read:

> Everything all right? You got the phone unplugged? The old man is on his way out. Get this: HE DOESN'T BELIEVE HE WILL DIE. He's probably right. But the band is ready. Champagne is on ice. He's a tough old bird. At the funeral he'll probably climb out of the coffin and box my ears. Either way, see you in a couple of weeks. Plug in the phone, will you?

The following morning a second postcard read:

> Father in coma. Don't send flowers. Probably playing possum. Hit the double at Birmingham yesterday. All you do is go to the paddock and find out which ones can walk. Maybe see you in a week?

In the pile was also a letter from a lady in Wales who was looking for bootlegs of Dylan. I hadn't run into many bootlegs and didn't know where to find them or what their values might be if I did. Shelly had no bootleg catalogues. I'd have to wait for his return on this one.

Tuesday number five running Shelly's business, eleven in the morning, Sweets with his head out the passenger window, I passed the Coco's. I passed the Coco's a lot more than I probably needed to. Inside there seemed to be an answer, even if I wasn't sure what the question was. On impulse, I pulled into the lot. Sweets gave me a woeful look.

You want something? I asked him. *Corn fritters?*

His front paws began to dance in anticipation. *How about a pancake?*

I'll do my best.

He grunted and sneezed. *And bacon.*

I brought some of the order forms in with me and the pricing catalogue to get a jump on the afternoon. The place was packed and I grabbed the only open table in the corner. I didn't see Renee at first, then she sprang through the doors with four plates balanced on her right arm. She moved at an impelled angle, harried, blowing air. I liked her hustle, the film of sweat on her brow, her personal dedication to a thankless job.

Again I was reminded in the way she moved of my Czech girl-friend long ago, the real love of my life that never had a chance of working out and probably suckered me into marrying an Asian girl. Asians were supposedly more loyal than other women, but it wasn't my fault the way I was, I recited to myself as the psychiatrists had instructed. My delusional, romantic worldview and great expectations factored in with my stunted development and propensity for chasing rainbows had left me like so many of my contemporaries with two handfuls of nothing.

Renee was not my waitress. My waitress was Ruby, mid-forties, rotund and slow, with improbably sculpted and heavily lacquered hair, as if she'd been issued from a country-western song or a seventies sitcom about a diner. Perhaps when she died she would not go to heaven but into syndication. I studied my price guide, scribbling down the titles I needed for the day. I reread Shelly's latest postcard, admiring his combination of flippancy and gravity, life's inevitable tragedy always turned into a punch-line with rim shot and cymbal crash.

Coco's was the corporate diner, and I was supposed to hate it, but it was twenty times better than the tater tots, corn dogs, hard stares, Styrofoam, mixed nuts, truculent clients, roaming staff, and cold calcified light of the cafeteria at Napa State.

The place began to thin out about one. I'd done all my early-bird work and was ready to leave. I'd hoped to talk with Renee, but she'd been too busy to notice, or maybe she didn't recognize me. She stood across the room talking to an older man, fifty or so, with spiky gray hair, a flushed complexion from drink, and a skull full of squeaking birds. In a loud slur, he was saying something about Carol McCoy and Ali McGraw.

"Yes, you told me that," Renee said.

"In *The Getaway*. We oughta get away."

"I have to work, Mr. Fromm."

"Call me Len." He reached for her arm. Renee looked about for help. This was the corporate diner, though, where none of us had any stake, including the employees.

I closed my guide.

"She was a lot better off when she was Mrs. Sam Peckinpah," he went on saying.

I wondered why such a superficial construct as Hollywood was so important to him.

Back in the Industrial Age when average life expectancy was forty-five years but restaurants were an extension of the community, three guys would've had Mr. Hollywood by the seat of his pants by now and on his way out to meet the sidewalk. In the Corporate Age, Renee sweated it out all alone in her nylon Coco's suit.

"Why don't you give me your number?" he said.

I rose and strode across the room. "Excuse me, *jefe*, but I don't like the way you are talking to this woman."

"Who are you?" he said.

"An escaped mental patient."

The squeaking in his head increased. I divined that he was poorly raised and preserved emotionally at around age eight. These types were rampant at Napa. Appeals were pointless. The only language the Mr. Peckinpahs of the world understood was violence. So I explained to him some of the things I'd picked up in Mudville, such as never initiate a fight from the sitting position, first punch usually wins, and the best way to get out of a headlock is to not get yourself in one in the first place. I added that if he wanted to wager fifty dollars on the contest, last man standing, I'd give him eight to five.

He stared at me for a while. It was so quiet in there you could hear the cod frying in the back. The manager bumped out the doors but just stood there.

"I don't fight anymore," he said. The truth we both knew was closer to, *I bluff and when called I fold.*

"Then you should probably get running," I replied.

Mr. Peckinpah cleared his throat, stood, harrumphed, thought to make a final remark but instead threw a twenty-dollar bill on the table and stalked scarlet-faced for the exits.

One diner actually clapped. The manager shrugged and returned to the kitchen. I went back to my table to get my things.

Renee followed. "Thanks," she whispered. "What was your name again?"

"Eddie. Eddie Plum."

"Thanks for getting me out of that, really. He comes in once a week, always drunk."

"Least I could do."

"Can I get you anything, another cup of coffee?"

Funny how I could still imagine, like Shelly, that day when the right girl would walk out of sunlight and change my life, as Sofia had. Probably all the sappy love songs I'd been listening to lately. I would have liked to have sat with her for a while, if only just to talk. There was something comforting about the familiarity of her face.

"If you could get me an order of pancakes with a side of bacon to go that would be great," I said.

She scribbled on her pad. "No problem. Hey, it's on me." Her eye caught my record guide. "You a record collector?"

"A dabbler."

She nodded as if I might have something to add.

"So many jerks out these days," I offered.

She tossed her head, blew a stream of air. "All morning I told myself I'd quit."

I imagined her kitchen, her television shows, the perfume on her dresser. "Well, you're about done for the day at least," I said. "Yes?"

"Just about, yes." She glanced at her watch, then gave me a nervous smile. There was a commotion in the kitchen. "Better go hang this ticket," she said.

As I walked back to my truck with the doggie bag full of pancakes and bacon it occurred to me where I'd seen Renee before. I drove back to Shelly's and unhooked the door of Donny's room. I stared at the photos for a long while. The girl in the cheerleader outfit, the girl with her hands on her knees, the girl in the tartan skirt, the girl in the smoky retouched photo framed inside the sequined heart on the television. A long time ago, Renee was Donny's girl.

24. *Zopilote* Being an Indian Word for "Vulture"

NOW THAT I HAD MONEY AGAIN, I BEGAN GOING DOWN TO TIJUANA to flit among the *puestos* and gambling salons, the *cantinas* and liquor stores, the oyster bars and *burdeles*. My Spanish had deteriorated, so it was a real challenge to amuse the prostitutes, who did not like me. Feeling bad afterward, I'd go to a church, usually Our Lady of Guadalupe, to pray and leave an offering. I wanted to be a good person, not a frantic bananacake buzzing around hot flesh like a housefly.

On one trip, thinking about these poor women disappearing, I drove toward the great smokestack of one of the world's largest landfills called simply by the locals *La Zona Basura*. I parked at the edge and looked down into the valley of discards, watched the great belly-roaring fire, the *zopilotes* getting their ankles muddy in the dog carcasses, the seagulls turning and screeling, and the garbage dwellers peeking out of their trash igloos. The lanes between the heaps of walruses and oyster shells and dining room tables teemed with autos and dashing urchins and people throwing their crap willy-nilly. Many were picking adroitly through the midden, filling burlap bags as fast as others were throwing it on. Six or seven lean, white-fanged mutts appeared to rule this netherworld. A thick column of raw smoke chugged upward from the hundred-meter copper chimney into the brownish Tijuana sky.

The wind shifted and a gust of smoke and decomposition blew into my face so acrid and foul that I had to cover my face with my arm. When the air cleared, I saw a garbage truck clamber down through the heaps and pull up alongside the incinerator. The passageway was so narrow the truck was forced in a little close for comfort. Twice the driver rang a bell. One of the white-fanged netherworld pups raised its snout and gave a long howl. The bucket then tipped, and as the truck turned and pulled away I saw in the firelight the scorch marks up the side of the passenger door, the same marks on Shelly's truck.

On the way back to the Island to pick up Sweets, who would chastise me for my Tijuana jaunt and my rubbish and prostitute smell, I stopped in at Shelly's house to see if he had returned. He should've been home long ago. The house felt different this morning and I found the door unlocked. I hoped that no one had broken in. The door as usual stuck slightly and it was dark inside. There was cash on the table in plain sight. I had not left the cash. I called and looked about. Whoever had been here was gone.

I'd been holding three Mexican beers since the border, so I raced down the hall. Out of habit I closed the bathroom door behind me. The bathroom was another furry chamber, moldy curtains and mildewed tile, toilet stained, vintage bachelor. There were a few vestiges of his "airhead" mom, a basketful of ancient soap balls, a homey plaque with cartoon rabbits. While I was peeing I heard voices. Just the stream hitting the water, I thought. When I stopped, the voices stopped. I stood for a minute, listening. Something brushed against the door. Quelling the urge to shout, I zipped up hastily, flushed, waved my hands under cold running water. In the mirror my eyes were zapped wide in my scarred and mangy penguin face. I fingered back my Streisand hair. Shelly has returned, I told myself, and is fooling around out there. I felt a cold fear opening the door, dusky hall, smell of fur, ink, dust, vague rot, sea.

No one was there.

Now the front door clunked open. I'm surrounded, I thought to myself. I've been set up. I considered turning back and scrambling out the bathroom window. But it was no stranger who came through the front door. It was a haggard Shelly, twelve pack under arm.

"When did you get back?" I said sharply, wiping the damp from my forehead with a sleeve.

"This morning," he said, setting the twelve pack on the table. He looked around, rubbed his head. He seemed dazed. I realized he'd been drinking. "You wanna beer?" he said.

"Is there someone here?" I said.

"What?" His head wobbled as he handed me a warm Miller Lite and glanced down the hall.

"I thought I heard someone. I was taking a whiz… Never mind."

He shook his head. "I called you when I got in."

"I was down in TJ."

"How'd everything go?" he said.

"Same as always," I said. "Whore, church, a few tacos."

"I mean my business."

"Oh, that. Fine. Good. You've got a great business."

"Thanks."

"Everyone wants 1960 America."

He offered a weak smile and took a haul off his beer.

"It was better then, wasn't it?" I said

"You can't blame Elvis," he said

"How was… Alabama?" I asked.

Again he glanced down the hall. "Oh, great, you know I'm mostly just burying people these days."

"Your father?"

"Yeah. To the last second he didn't believe he would die. What do you call that, a messianic complex?"

I opened my can.

There was that sound again, a wordless voice, almost a moan. It was my turn to glance down the hall. "You need to get out this house, boy," I said. "You got ghosts in here, you know that?"

He managed a smile that seemed to say: now you finally understand what I'm dealing with here.

"Well, I'd better get going," I said. "Got to get home and feed Sweets."

"All right, man." He followed me out and closed the door behind him as if he were trying to prevent rattlesnakes from escaping. Music was now playing inside. He yanked on the doorknob again and again.

At the gate I couldn't help wonder what kind of Alabama souvenir he'd brought home. Lover? Victim? Perhaps his father, who would not die but take his turn sitting in the cage? Or maybe it was the same guy as before, the megalocephalic special friend.

"Damn it," he said, more to himself than me. "I'm going to inherit this house. I hate this house."

"Sell it," I said.

"To the Nuremberg Museum," he said.

"Or you could have a bonfire. Invite all the neighbors."

"I'm going to inherit everything," he repeated in disbelief. He gazed at me, bedeviled, nothing like the festivity he'd imagined. "More paperwork than I know what to do with," he grumbled.

It's too much to ask, I thought. Your parents torture and disable you, then they die and leave you with all the *paperwork*.

"I have to go back," he said.

"Why?"

"Vultures."

"Who?"

"Lawyers and accountants."

"When?"

"Soon. A week or so."

25.   Flowers in the Sea

WHEN SHELLY RETURNED TO ALABAMA A WEEK LATER TO SETTLE his father's estate, I agreed to run his business. Sweets and I moved with a Bible and a bottle of brandy into that back room one more time. The house was in shambles, stacks of unwashed dishes and heaps of clothes all about. Shelly'd done little work restocking inventory or filling orders. He'd always looked upon his family situation as a Hollywood producer might a revenge formula, a story that rose sweetly on the fulcrum of injustice until the glorious and satisfying moment when the bad guys met their deservedly brutal end. But there had been no such satisfaction or justice for him. His parents had simply died, all chances of forgiveness and restitution were lost, and he was more alone in the world than ever.

The door to Donny's room was unlatched. Reluctantly, I entered. The bed was unmade. Someone had been sleeping here. And I knew that it was not Shelly. Sweets did not know who it might be, either. *It is an old smell,* he said, *the smell of a person all over the house.* I thought of Ed Gein, who'd flay his victims in order that he might one day be able to dress up in their skin.

The following day after hitting the swap meet and three garage sales (and landing a mint copy of "Wouldn't It Be Nice" by Johnny Rhythm and the Audios, 1961 on MGM, worth about sixty bucks), I drove to the old shell shop that stood above the Clam. A bell announced my arrival. The place was empty. The windows were like grape-blue photographs of choppy sea. There was the usual gift shop assortment of nautical bric-a-brac, cards, stained glass, shells, jewelry, model ships, brass barometers and sextants, somnolent volumes of photographs. The store had a ship's smell, canvas, old wood, varnish, and the faint rank of harbor seals. There were rental arrangements on various types of snorkel gear. A sign next to the register informed me that for five bucks I could navigate the old smuggler's tunnel that led to the ocean below and through which the bodies of the dead and maimed who jumped from the cliffs were brought.

A birdlike woman of about sixty appeared. She reminded me of a tern, so white and smooth with a needle nose and quick black eyes. "Can I help you?" she said.

I picked up a sand dollar. "I've recently learned about a boy who died here," I said, gesturing toward the cliff. "The brother of a friend of mine. And I wondered if you might remember him."

She folded her hands in front of her. "I used to keep track of them all," she said, tapping her famous book, "but I finally stopped. I thought for a time that if I stopped writing they'd stop coming." Her lips formed a prim imitation of a smile. "How long ago was it?"

"Oh, he would've been roughly my age. He was eighteen at the time. Somewhere around twenty-two years ago."

"What was his name?"

"Donald Hubbard. Donny Ray, they called him."

Her mouth turned down. She had a beautiful shop, rich in history, extraordinary view, some of the most valuable real estate on earth, but it was haunted by the cries of bleeding, drowning souls.

"I'd have that one," she said, opening the book. "Donny Ray…" She leafed through the pages, licking her thumb. There must've been thousands of names catalogued, her guestbook a gate book of children born suddenly into dark new worlds.

"Here he is," she said. "Donald Raymond Hubbard, July 3. I remember that one." She let out a withering sound, like the whinny of a horse. Her eyes rolled back and she closed the book. Her head seemed to float as she drifted to the southern windows. "I can see them jump from here." She pointed as if someone were standing out there now, poised to dive. "Donald was slim and dark," she said. "He looked like a dancer with his long legs and gleaming skin. He laughed before he jumped, I recall." She looked to me expectantly, as if I might understand. "Most are terrified. Others pretend they aren't. But Donny seemed to not be afraid. There were two with him, a young girl and an older, pale boy who sat up the bluff a ways. He was a bit of a sulker."

"Shelly?"

"I don't know their names. The pale boy was shouting and taunting, telling Donny to jump. He must've felt awful when he got his wish. The girl still comes from time to time, like so many, to throw flowers into the sea."

"The girl?" I said

"Yes. It was Donny's girlfriend, I believe. She came briefly when they brought Donny up through the tunnel into the ambulance. She was devastated, hysterical. To watch someone you love end up like that…" Her glasses had slid to the tip of her nose. She pushed them back. "It tears your heart out, doesn't it?"

26.   It Ain't Goldilocks

WHEN I PULLED INTO THE COCO'S LOT RENEE WAS WALKING out the door. It was too early for her shift to be up. She looked tense, though she always moved as if a stiff wind were at her tail. I was pretty sure she had quit and this might be the last time I would see her. By the time I'd circled back around she was squealing out of the driveway in her red Nissan Sentra. I followed. She drove as if she were in a motor race, passing recklessly, jockeying and tailgating as she got bottled up in the left lane.

The air cooled as we moved west, the clouds disintegrating as they made their charge inland. My old Ford was a six cylinder and needed a tune-up. I had trouble staying up. I almost lost her several times.

She took the Old Town exit, swept away south around Presidio Park, driving as if she knew she were being followed. I lost her finally on Rosecrans. I felt like an inept television detective.

Which way should I go? I asked Sweets.

Heck if I know. I just wish you'd slow down. Do you want me to puke?

I've got to find her. I need to know about Donny.

Turn down the radio, can you? And would you wind down the window? It's hot in this cab.

I turned off the radio and rolled the window down, continuing to wander through the Point Loma neighborhoods under the shadow of Donny and Renee's romance. What would it be like to watch your first love broken below on the rocks? Could you ever be the same again? Would you ever be able to love again?

I hung a left and a left and a left, imagining Donny and Renee at Baskin-Robbins. I imagined their first awkward kiss. I imagined the first time they made love. Over and over, I saw Donny Ray lying on the rocks and Renee throwing flowers into the sea. Then I saw Renee's Sentra parked along the curb. I pulled in behind it and got out. I stood on the grass for a moment, arms akimbo, looking around.

"Hey!"

I looked up to see her on a balcony, scowling down at me. "Are you stalking me?"

"I tried to catch you at Coco's," I replied. "You left early."

"Just because you rescue me from some old drunk doesn't mean you get to follow me home."

"I only want to ask you one question."

"About what?"

"About Donny Hubbard."

Her head jerked and she stared at me in profile through her fallen hair. The top button of her uniform was undone. "Donny?" She seemed suddenly out of breath. "Did you know him?"

"I know his brother."

"Shelly?" She gripped the rail. "How do you know Shelly?"

"From the racetrack. I'm watching his business. Do you mind if I come up?"

"I don't know." She fastened the button. "Did you really escape from a mental hospital?"

"Yes."

"Why were you there?"

"I lost my wife, and then I lost my mind."

She licked her lips. "I have to be at my second job in an hour."

"It won't take a minute."

"I don't even know you."

"One question."

She looked away. "I'm in apartment 21."

Renee's two-bedroom apartment had an old round brown couch, brown shag carpeting, a few bland seascapes in driftwood frames on the walls. There were two green-gold barrel recliners and an antique trunk with castors for a coffee table. The kitchen was small, bright, with a glass table inside. There were pictures of children all around, two boys, roughly as Shelly described. Their father was nowhere represented. Renee perched herself on the edge of a green recliner. "What do you want to know about Donny?" she demanded.

"Just one thing. Is he still alive?"

"No, he's not." Her lips tightened. She clutched her collar. She blinked rapidly and pressed together her knees. "Why do you ask?"

"I'm watching Shelly's house and his business," I explained. "Both his parents have died and he's had to go back to Alabama."

Renee, huddled, watched me through narrowed eyes. "I'm surprised he let you in," she said.

"You know Donny's room hasn't changed in twenty years. But there are sounds from that room that I can't explain. There is a tape marked 'Donny's Favorite Songs: 1986.' Someone sleeps in his bed, and I'm pretty sure it isn't Goldilocks. Whenever I'm in that house alone I don't feel like I'm alone. Shelly is hiding something."

She cast a glance to the side. "That's Shelly for you."

"I checked back through all the obituaries of that year and Donny is not listed."

She relaxed a bit. Her arms unfolded from her chest. "That's because he didn't die here."

"Where did he die?"

She shut her eyes and explored with her fingertip the cup of her throat. "He was in a coma for so long they finally took him back to Alabama." Now she stood and began to pace. "It was a miracle that he lived at all. God." She looked up at the ceiling. "I went to see him once before they took him back. They had him in Spring Valley at a convalescent hospital. His eyes were open. One arm had shrunk up into his chest."

Her face was drawn now, and she shook her head for a good thirty seconds, eyes closed. "When I heard that he finally died, I hate to say it but it was a relief." Moving to the window she looked out for a while before speaking again. "I know he'll forgive me for saying that."

"I'm sorry to bring it all up again."

She took a deep breath. "I still dream about him. Sometimes I swear he's still around, watching over me. Maybe he's visiting you too."

"Maybe so."

She sat again at the edge of her chair. "How long has Shelly been your friend?"

"I met him at the Del Mar Racetrack when I was seventeen."

"You're a record-collecting buddy?"

"Horseracing buddy, mainly."

"You'd be the first friend of Shelly's I ever met." She flapped her lashes at me. "He keeps them all a secret."

"Why does he come to see you every Tuesday?"

She snorted and her lip curled. "He used to tag along with Donny and me, I mean everywhere, movies, beach—four years older than Donny and he was more like the little brother. He was jealous of Donny because Donny had everything Shelly didn't—good looks, confidence, athletic ability, *girl*friends. Shelly loved music but Donny could play."

"I see."

She studied me a while, the lashes of her pale eyes flickering. She stretched out an ankle, lifted her hair from her neck and said after a minute: "When he came along with us that day to the Clam, Donny had no plans to jump. That was Shelly's idea. Of course *Shelly* wasn't going to jump. He used to taunt Donny sometimes—he liked to egg him on—and he started in with this little chant. *Jump, boy, jump.* Donny was athletic and could swim pretty well, and I think he wanted to show Shelly, to prove something or whatever, you know, like little brothers will do. Anyway, Donny could dive off a three-meter board, but he never went off anything high as the Clam, with rocks below and the waves going in and out." She pulled her front lip under her bottom teeth and her eyebrows plunged. "I told him not to. He wasn't turned right. Instead of just jumping he tried to dive. I thought he was dead the minute he went off." She covered her face and let out a wail. "God, it was horrible."

I let her cry. I wanted to leave, but Renee took a deep breath and continued. "Shelly's always *liked* me," she said, marking the word "liked" in quotes with her fingers. "After Donny died he kept calling me up, trying to get together. I'd change jobs and he'd find me again. When I got married he disappeared for a while, but now that I'm divorced he's back again."

It occurred to me that Shelly might've wanted on some level to be rid of his brother so he could have Renee to himself, the possibility might have seemed more than a fantasy to him then, but I took the high road. "Maybe he just wants to be forgiven."

"I won't ever forgive him." She wrenched her head side to side, her makeup streaked from tears. "He killed Donny."

27. My Boy Lollipop

ONE DAY AT A GARAGE SALE IN POWAY I FOUND A 78-FORMAT BEATLES single of "Please Please Me," pressed in India on Parlophone Records. Several countries continued to press 78s long after the format was obsolete. The records were almost unheard of. The lady was liquidating the collection of her son, who was going to prison for four years on an embezzlement charge. Lucky lad, they weren't sending him to Napa State. She understood that a Beatles record might be valuable and felt that ten dollars was a fair price. It might've been worth upwards of five thousand. I paid her the ten and hoped it wasn't a counterfeit.

Immediately I drove to Shelly's house to show him. His truck was not out front, but the lights were on and I heard music playing inside. As I got closer I recognized the song "My Boy Lollipop," Millie Small (the Blue Beat Girl) on Smash Records, 1964, released in Europe on Fontana, one of the few ska hits in the history of early pop music, worth about ten bucks in good condition, and it was really blasting.

Curiosity aroused, I knocked. No answer. *You make my heart gooo giddy-yup.* "Shelly?"

You ah my one de-siah.

I knocked again.

The door opened a crack. It was that same single eye peering down on me. The hair bristled on the back of my neck.

"Shelly?" I shouted over the music. "Is that you?"

The door opened wider. The figure before me was thin and stooped and wore a rubber Ronald Reagan mask and a pin-striped, oversized New York Yankees jersey. There were several gold chains hanging from his neck. An elaborate gold watch had slid down his skinny arm to the back of his hand. His other arm was shrunken into his chest. For a moment I thought the rickety caricature before me must be a joke, Shelly in Halloween garb. "Shelly?"

"Come on in, negro," said the hollow voice inside the mask.

I need ya I need ya I need ya soooo.

No one had ever called me "negro" before, not even in the nuthouse. "Is Shelly here?" I pressed.

"No, Chuck ain't here," came the reply.

Bap Bap: my boy lollipop.

"I'm a friend of his," I explained. "I've found a Beatles record on Parlophone. I was wondering… is he around?"

The figure tipped his head at me in what initially suggested curiosity until I realized he was inclined this way by the arrangement of his spine.

"Do you know when he'll be back?"

"Any minute. Went to Gag in the Bag."

You make my heart gooo giddy-yup.

He lifted the hand with the watch on it, then swung the door completely out and limped away, dragging his left leg behind him, his carriage popping up like the weasel in the children's song every other step. I followed looking around for Shelly the mad scientist. Murdered probably. I had finally stumbled into one of his Taboo Zones. A glass eye peered up at me from Shelly's work table, the iris in it brown. The arm of the record player kicked over, rested for a moment, then swung back and dropped again into the groove. *Bap Bap: My boy lollipop.*

"Do you mind?" I said, lifting the stylus from Millie Small and switching off the player.

I heard a car door slam outside, the gate creaking, now the sounds of footsteps up the walk, hard soles. Ronald Reagan retreated to the foot of the hall. The sun did its best to penetrate the grime of the ancient curtains. The front door clunked open. Expressionless, Shelly looked back and forth between us, two white Jack in the Box bags in his hand. His tone was plaintive. "Donny, I thought I told you not to answer the door."

Donny's head fell, which made him all the more hunched looking, the delicate paralyzed hand pressed into his body almost chin high.

"He didn't," I said. "I came in. I heard the record playing over and over. I thought something was wrong."

"It's cool, Chuck," said Donny.

Shelly nodded, sighed, closed the door behind him with his right foot. He set the bags of food on the kitchen counter. The strong odor of hamburgers, onions, and French fries drifted to my nose. "Why don't you go to your room, Donny?" Shelly said. "Go on. I need to talk to Eddie for a minute."

"Am I in trouble?"

"No, nothing like that."

The mask nodded and Donny turned and dragged away, rising each time his weight shifted from the dead leg to the ball of his good foot.

Shelly drifted around idly picking things up and then took a chair at his work table with the glass eye looking up at him, crossed his arms over his chest and said, "So now you've met my brother. Like I told you, I inherited everything."

"Why did you tell me he was dead?"

"Long story."

"And the mask?"

"If he took it off you'd understand."

"He called me a negro."

"He worked with black people."

"He worked?"

"Yeah, until recently he was a janitor."

"I heard he died in Alabama."

"Who told you that?"

"Renee."

His eyes widened. "Renee?"

"She said he was in a coma for two years."

"Yeah." He rubbed the back of his neck, then creaked back and forth in his chair, straining his neck up as if he were trying to swallow a nail. "From the beginning every last doctor said he wouldn't live. After a year my father wanted to pull the plug. He finally got his wish." Shelly cradled his head, appearing to weather a wave of migraine. "After they took him off life support everyone presumed he would die. But Donny lived. My mother took care of him. My father told everyone that Donny had died. It was just easier that way. When Donny got better, he got a job and moved into a little trailer not far from my folks."

"I see."

"You know he broke his skull in fifteen places. He can't remember anything. He's proof to me that there is no God."

I looked up and Donny was standing in the hall.

"Hello, Donny Ray," I said.

"Hello, negro," he returned.

Shelly picked up the 78 copy of "Please Please Me" and held it to the light. His hands were shaking. "Never even saw one of these before. Where'd you find it?"

"Garage sale in Poway."

"Helluva score. You want a beer?"

"No thanks. I gotta go. Dog's in the car."

"I'll give you a call."

28. KLIK in Canoga Park

SHELLY CALLED ME UP TWO DAYS LATER. "I GOTTA GO UP TO L. A. for an auction," he said. "KLIK in Canoga Park went belly-up. You wanna come?"

"I don't know, man."

"It's a public auction."

"Yeah, I read about it."

"Lots of dupes and promos, posters, autographed stuff, everything. Like a year's worth of garage sales in one day."

"Donny coming?"

"Yeah. Last time I left him alone he broke a Shirelles record and ate a whole chocolate cake."

"Shirelles aren't worth much," I said.

"He gets kind of lonesome, too," he said. "He's used to my mom being around."

"Does he know she's gone?"

"He was at the funeral. But I don't believe he remembers."

"Does he remember you're his brother?"

"Oh yeah."

"Why does he call you Chuck?"

"You tell me, babe."

"What does he like to talk about? What does he do?"

"He likes music. He's a big Yankees fan. For a while he knew all the planets and the nearby stars and that kind of stuff. His hobby is buying life insurance. These hucksters come around, the door-to-door guys you still see in the South, and sell him wacky policies. He's bought forty or fifty of them, one of them if he dies of melanoma before he's forty-five pays out like three million."

"Everyone should have a hobby," I said. "Okay, I'll go with you. Maybe we can catch half a card at Hollypark."

"Del Mar's opening in a week, believe it?"

"I haven't looked at a *Form* in a month."

"Me neither."

"What's happened to us?"

"Old age, I guess. I'll pick you up at the Island in an hour."

29.   Boys Love Their Mothers

WE DROVE UP TO L.A. THREE ABREAST IN SHELLY'S SCORCHED Nissan. Donny was not wearing his mask. His head was an inflamed quilt of overlapping scars. He was hard to look at, but he looked exactly like what he was, a boy who had jumped thirty feet off a sea cliff face first into a bed of rocks. The disproportion of his features was centered around a lighting-white scar that ran from deep in the scalp all the way down to his chin. The facial halves were so poorly matched that the sightless eye sat a good inch below the good one. Several front teeth were missing and the remaining incisors curled downward giving him a vampirish aspect. His sparse hair was clumped into a peak like a mohawk. His thoughts peeped out, a scramble of *mommy, mommy* and *will you love me tomorrow*. Boys love their mothers, I thought. Too bad I never really had one.

From Del Mar the radio station in Canoga Park was eighty miles or so. We sat in silence, only the radio talking. Donny said finally, "My brain hurts."

"Where's your eye at, Donny?" asked Shelly.

"In my pocket."

"Put it in."

"I can't see through it."

"You need to wear it or you'll lose it again."

"It itches."

"Put it in."

Donny's hand groped about in his pocket, but he didn't withdraw the eye. Instead he turned the raw and vacant aperture upon me.

"How about those Yankees?" I said.

"Who?" said Donny.

"The New York Yankees."

"Oh, them, yeah."

"I think they're in first place," I said.

"Well, I'll be dipped," he said.

"Too bad they didn't keep Chili Davis," I said.

"Good Old Chili," said Donny.

The traffic thickened briefly and Shelly downshifted. "That Beatles record is not a counterfeit," he said.

"How much is it worth?"

"Four thousand, maybe more."

"I think I'll keep it."

"I would too," he said.

"So would I," said Donny Ray.

30.   Try a Little Tenderness

ONLY ABOUT FIFTY BIDDERS SHOWED UP FOR THE AUCTION IN a meeting hall at the old KLIK radio station in Canoga Park. The owner of KLIK, an oldies format overrun by time, wanted to liquidate immediately, so except for promotional records and a few autographed items, most of the inventory was being sold off in bulk. The owner had five other radio stations, every one moving to a more profitable pre-recorded format, with America falling asleep between the commercials.

I was bewildered by the patter of the auctioneer, square dancing had never been my forte, and since this was Shelly's trip and I was not going to compete with him I sat back and watched. Shelly had his game face on and was picking up box after box for almost nothing. Though most of the bidders seem baffled by his enthusiasm, I knew he was racking up the score. Dinah Shore, even with Sinatra, was worth nothing until you pushed her across the golden threshold into Japan.

Though most of the participants were as focused as Shelly, there was the occasional alarmed glance in our direction. Donny without his mask was indeed a marvelous spectacle, like a gruesome alien out of *Star Trek*. After twenty minutes Donny got restless in his metal chair, so I suggested we go out into the lobby for a while and stretch our legs. "Can he drink pop?" I asked Shelly.

"Yeah, but watch him. He'll spill it."

Donny was fascinated by the 1940s modernist theme of the lobby, brass chip floor, coarse black-pebbled walls, a swooping Bauhaus ceiling with many hexagonal skylights. Along one wall was a row of black and white faces, celebrities mostly who'd stopped in at some time to pitch their wares on KLIK radio. I stopped before a photo of Eddie Cochran, whose voice breaks in "Three Stars," his posthumously released tribute to Buddy Holly, J. P. Richardson, and Richie Valens, all of whom preceded him in death by one year. Even if his look and pose are all Elvis, Eddie was an original, "proto punk" as they called it now, killed by a negligent taxicab driver named George Martin, coincidentally the same name as the man who "discovered" and produced the Beatles. When the British invaded America four years later, all the great American rockers were dead or gone. Elvis had enlisted, and there was no one but Motown to stop them.

Donny surveyed the portraits, then leaned in to study a gauzy promo image of Otis Redding. I'd never known much about Otis Redding, the only songs of his I'd been familiar with were the overplayed "The Dock of the Bay," The Black Crowes cover "Hard to Handle," and the Three Dog Night version of his "Try a Little Tenderness," but I'd picked up a number of his singles and LPs in the last few months and gained admiration. He was one of those double-coupon artists whose value rewards both the pocket and the ear. If you really wanted to "invest" in music, as well as ward off the zombies of the corporate age, both Shelly and I agreed, soul was the way to go.

"Do you know who that is, Donny?" I said, pointing to Otis Redding.

"Looks like Ernesto," he said.

"Who's Ernesto?"

"He runs the scrubber."

"It's Otis Redding. Remember that song, 'Try a Little Tenderness'?"

"Oh, yeah."

He didn't remember. I wanted him to be a whiz kid, a genius—I wanted him to instantly count spilled toothpicks like Rain Man or calculate Martian orbital eccentricities or pontificate on the golden ratio, but those rocks at the bottom of the Clam had given him little back but the thread of his life.

We strolled down the curved halls and I looked for a pop machine. "Maybe they've auctioned them off already," I mumbled. "You tired? You want to sit for a minute?"

Donny Ray sat, out of breath, his mashed head sagging, his thin arms folded over his chest. His breathing was shallow. "We'll wait for Shelly here," I said.

"Where are we, anyway?" he asked.

"Los Angeles, California."

"Hmmm," he said. "Is Mom here?"

"You don't remember the funeral?"

He raised his head, turning his empty eye socket upon me. "Oh, yeah."

He didn't remember the funeral.

"Do you remember Renee, Donny?"

His head flicked to the left, then to the right. His fingers entwined into his gold chains, his raw sightless eye drifted over me. He grew very still.

"I saw her the other day," I said, and thought of my own lost love, Sofia, her picture shimmering up before me. "She says she still thinks of you."

His hand had wandered into the pocket where he kept his prosthetic eye. He scratched his ear, hitched a sob, and said, "I remember her."

Shelly came striding around the corner, looking peeved. "Hey, I been looking for you guys all over. Come on, they're loading my truck out back. Let's get out of here, maybe we can catch the fifth at Hollypark."

"I remember," Donny announced to his brother, getting to his feet. "I loved her."

Shelly gave me a look as if I'd been trying to sell his brother drugs.

"I remember now," Donny repeated, looking up at the skylights.

"That's right, Donny," said Shelly. "Come on, let's get out of here."

31.   Will You Still Love Me Tomorrow?

I WOKE UP ONE MORNING TO THE SOUND OF SCREAMING, THINKING at first it was Beatriz or a peafowl in a tree. When I went outside the Island grounds were festooned with paper flowers and balloons. Picnic tables and a bandstand had been set up and *parillas* were stoked and lit. A pig, the screamer, lay yonder, hanging split by its back feet from a tree as a young man addressed it with a long curved knife. Two butter-brown girls with bows in their hair were playing jacks at the foot of my stairs.

"*¿Hola, que tal?*" I said to them. "*¿Que tenemos?*"

"*¡Es una fiesta!*" they cried in unison. "*¡Mataron un cochino!*"

"*¿Para que?*" I inquired.

"*¡El hipódromo!*" they shouted.

Every horse track has its pre-opening day celebration. Del Mar's was usually the best. As a child I recalled them, for all the children and good food and fun, more fondly than Christmas. For the last two weeks track employees, tourists, and gamblers had been pouring into Solana Beach and Del Mar, and rents everywhere had soared. I noted that all the *casitas* were now occupied and there were several new camp dogs. From below drifted the scent of warm hay and horse dung mingled with the ocean. A bugle sounded and there was the wet flank whack of horse flesh. A woman with an apron tied around her middle came down the stairs from cabin number 3 with a covered basket and two boys about twelve sailed on past toeing a black-and-white checkered soccer ball.

Past the lone orange tree in the distance blazed a great wood fire upon which sat a bubbling black cauldron. A perspiring man with a red bandana tied round his head wrung long sheets of pig skin, fed them with tongs into the hot fat, and then stacked the crackled lengths of *chicharron* longwise in a steel rack like so much cordwood.

Down the way I found Beatriz making *carnitas* in a large iron skillet over one of the fires, pouring over the frying cubes of pork a sauce made from Coca-Cola, ketchup, and chili vinegar. Her green parrot Paco was perched on the deck nearby, happily cackling the only two phrases it knew: *hijole chingao* and *todos los marinos son putos.* There was meat everywhere, the carnage of carnival and purple carcass majesty, ribs in pans, heaps of brains and tripe, snout and feet, head and back meat, side meat already frying and headed for *frijoles charros*, chops and hams and scraps galore for Sweets and his pals.

By noon, a full-fledged fiesta was underway. A *guitarrista* and an accordion player named Poka had started up on the podium. A pickup truck with about nine men in its bed and more hanging off the running boards sputtered up the hill. The whooping passengers leapt off and began to unload cases of Tecate and Pacifico. All the *parillas* blazed with bright red coals, their mesquite and hickory smoke lifting to the clearing sky, and the best parts of the dressed pork, the *chuletas* and *lomo*, laid on the flames with whole chilies and onions and *nopales* still with their spines. Women kept appearing from the *casitas* with more food, *bolillos*, stacks of warm tortillas, cans of chipotles and bowls of chopped cilantro and onions and jars of salsa. Great galvanized tubs full of ice were stuffed with orange and lime *Jarritos* for the kiddies.

A guy with a trumpet appeared and for laughs blew the "Call to Post," then he and the *guitarrista* and Poka segued into *mariachi*. Beatriz now finished with the *carnitas* had soaked corn husks and with the freshly rendered pork fat was kneading a pile of *masa* for tamales. She waved me in. I did not cook, I told her. *Ahora si*, she said, and showed me how to spread the *masa* into the wet *hojas* and fill them with *adobada* and roll them. We laid them thirty at a time in a big steamer. As more revelers arrived, the music outside grew louder. A freshly caught shark was thrown onto the grill. Someone handed me a cold can of Tecate and I heard Sweets laughing and then saw his smartass face in the door.

I thought you didn't cook, he scoffed. *You lazy bastard. Look how happy you are.*

And it was true. I didn't know why. Memories and Del Mar

opening and these sweet familial people, many as illegal as me. I finished another beer, followed by two shots of tequila with a hot walker named Salvador who traveled with the circuit and knew my father well and even remembered me. This Salvador, he insisted I get drunk, and he talked about the days when he cooled the horses in the sea, but I did roll and steam about a hundred tamales, some with mangos and pineapples, before I slipped out of the grasp of Beatriz, and then I briefly played goalie in a soccer game and was scored on umpteen times by children and adults half my size, then I lost all my money in a dice game, followed by a violent discussion about thoroughbreds in which it was denied by several that I could possibly be the inventor of the Plum Variable, giving the credit instead to my father.

I had never danced and always refused to dance, but now I was dancing in circles with some *chiquita* with a face like intervention. It was only on *Sabado de Gloria*, the fiesta before Easter, when an effigy of a U.S. president was burned or blown up on general principles, but someone had an extra George W. Bush hanging around and to rousing cheers up in flames he went.

Late afternoon the wind shifted and the air grew lazy and warm. A boy like a maypole spun a lasso around himself. Now here came Shelly's pickup jostling up the trail, Donny on the passenger side waving from the open window. I gestured them up the hill as if I were flagging in an airship. Donny was nearly out of the truck before it stopped and let out a crazy yee-haw through the mouth of his rubber Ronald Reagan mask.

Shelly, looking a year older each time I saw him, climbed wearily out shaking his head. He looked all around. "Can't believe it's opening day at Del Mar tomorrow. First time I'll miss it in more than twenty years."

"Oh, well," I said, and steered him to the beer.

Shelly and I stood off to the side, he wearing a wry smile and holding a pulled pork torta in his left hand, a can of Tecate in his right. Donny in the meantime had joined the festivities. Considering that the effigy of a U.S. president had just been burned, and figuring in the Immigration Reform and Control Act of 1986, Ronald Reagan, I thought, fared rather well. Donny danced with the same woman I had, a very generous soul, the kind I should've married instead of Fang-Hua. Maybe my life would've turned out differently if I had, or if Sofia hadn't jumped from that window, but it was too late for all that.

Donny limped over to us after a while panting, the collar of his shirt wet from perspiration. "I want a beer, too," he said.

Shelly rolled his eyes. "You can't, babe. You're not old enough."

"How old am I, anyway, Chuck?"

"You're forty-one."

Donny clapped his hands together and scrubbed them around. The paralyzed hand was as pliant as the handle of a wooden walking cane. "Too young to drink," he crowed.

"How about just a paper cup?" I said. "Come on, it's a party. They'll be breaking up soon. They all have to get up at four."

Shelly gave me a glance.

"Can he drink?" I pressed. "I mean, are we saving him for some occasion?"

"He's got brain damage."

"So have I."

"All right, all right."

For Donny to drink he had to take off his mask. With some effort and a little help from Shelly, he peeled it away, a *Mission Impossible* moment. He blinked in the light. His good eye was rimmed with crud. As usual, he was not wearing his false eye. Shelly patted Donny's face with a napkin and tried to fluff out his thin and matted hair. Donny resisted his brother's attentions. There were many nervous glances in our direction. One younger girl stared greedily, the melting ice cream from her cone dripping down her wrist.

"Put your eye in," Shelly ordered. "You don't want your socket to fill up with lint."

Donny plugged the eye in as if he were putting a quarter into a vending machine. The good eye fluttered as if it had caught a gnat.

Except for a massive belch, Donny did all right with two cups of beer. He grooved on the *mariachi*, gnawed on a sandwich, stared into a blazing *parilla*, swung and missed a few times at a *piñata*, kicked a soccer ball, and let the kid with the lasso rope him around the waist. At one point a large silver sombrero was placed on his head. The brim of the hat was wider than his shoulders and Donny was so pleased with it he kept feeling for it to make sure it was still there.

Evening fell. The sun, merged in clouds, lingered just above the horizon. The passenger train that passed between the ocean and the track every hour or so appeared from around the bend. Bukowski wrote a poem about this train once, "THACK THACK THACKA" it went. He had his pint and needed eight teeth pulled and he was wearing his dead father's pants and I bet he missed the double and lost fifteen dollars that day. The shore was curtained in mist so the silver-blue train appeared to be emerging from a cloud.

And then the sun was gone and I was very drunk but content in a lawn chair with Sweets sitting at my feet. I watched Donny frolicking with the two girls at my porch that morning who were letting him fly their metallic green June bug attached to a string. Shelly strolled up wearing that serene expression that always came after five or six beers. He had a plateful of macaroni salad. He took the chair next to mine. "I'm taking Donny back to Alabama," he said, after a few bites. "I'm going to put him in a home. I can't take care of him and we have family there and it will be cheaper too."

"Too bad," I said.

"Wherever he goes now he does well."

"He seems fragile to me," I said.

"I hope this is my last Bay Minette trip," he said, getting a mouthful of macaroni. "Hey, Donny!" he called.

Donny wandered over, holding down his hat as if the wind might steal it. He looked like a rakish, spine-twisted, one-eyed Howdy Doody. "Mom is in heaven," he said.

"That's right, Donny. Go pee now. We got a long drive ahead of us."

32.   Whiplash I Was Taking a Bath

AFTER SHELLY LEFT TO TAKE DONNY BACK TO ALABAMA I WATCHED his business once more. He did not bother to leave me any order forms or petty cash, not a single comment, bit of advice, or cross remark about the Japanese. Two weeks passed before an actual letter arrived, written on blue-ruled paper in his big round style.

> Eddie: Found a place for Donny with our Aunt Floss, not really an aunt but a second cousin who lives in Carrollton (north). She lives alone in a big house that my grandfather built. Donny likes her, even if Donny likes everyone. I think it will work out. After I took him to the cemetery to show him Mom's and Dad's graves he said that he was going to die too, but I know humans can't simply die because they want to die. If we could I would've done it long ago. Ha ha. He says they're in heaven now, which shows that he has no memory of what they were like, but he is eating again pretty well so he had enough energy to make the trip. I think he will be all right. I'm headed home tomorrow. Need to get out of the South. Think I am allergic to rednecks and black-eyed peas. See you in three days.

Shelly didn't return, however, in three days. It was well over a week before I saw him again. I was in the record room with Sweets sorting through the bundles of records that he had bought at the KLIK auction and never bothered to open. It was a fabulous haul, a year's worth of revenue. Many duplicates, and many routine ten-dollar discs, but that's what you need when the same people want the same records over and over. There were a few jackpots too: a seven-inch single of "Kissing in the Dark" by Memphis Minnie on J.O.B. Records worth about three hundred and Tom Crook and the Rock 'n Roll Four's "Weekend Boogie" on Dixie worth close to a grand.

The record-room window was open, and before I heard a car pull up in the driveway, Sweets said, *Shelly's here.*

There was talking, and I heard Shelly's muffled thanks. I thought, well, he's brought someone with him again, or maybe it's Donny because Aunt Floss didn't work out. I heard the car door closing, then the gate squeaking open. Looking out the open louvered windows, I saw a taxi pulling away. The front door whacked shut and Shelly appeared at the foot of the hall wearing a neck brace and a bandage on his elbow. Sweets and I went down to greet him. Stripes of sunlight from the open door fell across his upper body. His face had changed. He looked around as if he might've not known his own house.

"What happened?" I asked

He sniffed and took a seat at his work table. He wore this disconcertingly open but dazed expression.

"I was on my way back from Bay Minette," he said, fingering his brace. "I decided to drive in the day because I was almost run off the road the last time by a truck hauling chickens." He smiled in a way that only people in neck braces can. "It was eleven in the morning and I was going down highway 98 at sixty-five miles an hour, not far out from Mobile, when an old woman in a '67 Ford Galaxy pulled out in front of me. She had a face like a dried apricot. Her mouth was open. She had these big moronic eyes." He laughed, as if it were not only a distant but also a fond memory. "My foot never made the brake pedal. I didn't even have time to think about dying." He licked his lips. "Just before we collided—I saw the next world."

"No," I said.

He grinned at me. "I saw it, babe." He wiped at the air in circles with the heel of his hand. "You were right."

"I was?"

He was so tranquil and glowing it was unsettling. I'd known many people who'd gone through religious transformations, usually because their lives were out of control. This experience seemed genuine.

"What happened to the old lady?" I asked

He laughed. "Our cars were totaled. I mean we're both just sitting there with steering wheels in our hands and the rest of what we rode in on in pieces a mile down the road. Neither of us was wearing a seatbelt.

Neither of us was hurt. You should've seen her expression." He squeaked in absurd delight.

"She must've been Catholic," I said.

He squeaked again, grabbing his stomach. "Easy on me, babe."

"You got a little whiplash."

"Yeah, and some bruised ribs and a scratch on my arm. But that's it!" He held up the arm. "It was a miracle."

"How'd you get home?"

"I took the bus. I was in the hospital three days. Am I dreaming, Eddie?"

"How would I know?"

"Am I a ghost? Are we ghosts, Eddie?"

"Would my hair be cut like this if we were?"

"I keep thinking about the next world."

"What's it like?"

"It was the first time I ever felt loved." Despite the brace, he kept tipping his head, as if he could hear the music of that world where he'd felt for the first time loved. "I didn't want to come back until I saw my old man standing down at the end there with a golf club. He hated golf." He laughed until his eyes were wet.

"Did you see your life flash before your eyes?"

"Thank God, no!"

"And you didn't have any insurance?"

He waved his hand at me with a wince as he had to quell the habit of flipping aside his hair. "It doesn't matter. None of that shit I worried about all my life matters."

"What are you going to do?"

"I don't know," he said, wondrously. "I keep thinking about those goddamn little sparrows flying into the orange tree in your window. All my life that was me, a little sparrow flying over and over into a goddamn window. I'm done with that now." A giggle like a hiccup erupted from his throat.

"What about your business?"

He threw down his hand. "Take it if you want it. I don't ever want to see another piece of mail from Japan again."

"Tell me something. I've got to know."

"What is it? Anything, man."

"About the Tijuana prostitutes."

"The what?"

"The missing prostitutes whose bones were found in the incinerator at La Zona Basura."

He stared at me a while incredulously. "What are you talking about?"

"I couldn't help but notice the articles that you'd clipped for your killer scrapbook."

"Yeah?"

"And the burn marks up your door. I saw the same markings on another truck that pulled away from the incinerator at the dump in Tijuana."

"Yeah, I go there all the time, babe," he said, lifting his palms. "It's free, man. They charge you to burn your trash at the landfill here."

"Right, of course, right. Just thought maybe…"

"Thought maybe what? That I was killing them?"

"Why else would you snip the articles?"

"I thought it was you, babe."

33. Mister Jang-Jingler (Dance)

HEAD ON MY ARMS ON THE CUSHIONED BAR AT MOBY DICK'S, Tuesday afternoon, just me and Soo and a couple of men down the way dressed like Jackie Kennedy, both wearing blood-spattered double-breasted pink Chanel wool jackets and matching pillbox hats. The news was on the big TV up in the corner. They were running the Tijuana prostitute story again with alternating shots of bordellos and the big chimney at *La Zona Basura*. A few moments later Dr. Horace Jangler, my old bogus psychiatrist, was standing in front of a weather map indicating a low-pressure system with the sweep of his hand.

"Can you turn that up, Soo?" I said.

"Weather never change here," she grumbled, turning up the volume with the remote.

"I know that guy. How long has he been the Channel Eight weatherman?"

"All look same to me," she said with a shrug. "You want one more?"

"Yeah, can I use your phone?"

She placed the telephone and a directory on top of the bar. I looked up the number of Channel Eight.

"He can't come to the phone now," was the reply when I asked if I could talk to the weatherman.

"Will you leave him a message?"

"Of course."

"Tell him Willie Wihooley wants to see him."

"Wihooley."

"Yeah." I spelled it for her. "Tell him I'm at Moby Dick's. Tell him it's urgent. I'll wait for him."

"Moby Dick's?"

"Yeah, it's a bar, in Del Mar."

"Okay."

I replaced the receiver and turned to the door as if Jangler might have the power to instantly materialize. It was an hour and a half before he strolled through the whale's mouth, still wearing his weatherman suit. He was larger than I recalled and his gray locks were shorn. He moved briskly with an emphatic gunslinger swing of the shoulders.

"By golly, Willie Wihooley, it's good to see you," he said, grinning broadly and extending a hand. We had an enthusiastic handshake.

"Dr. Jangler," I returned. "You're a sight for sore eyes."

"I'm Dr. Jingler now," he said. "With each new incarnation I like to change a vowel."

"Well that's just fine," I said. "I hope you never run out of vowels. Let me buy you a drink."

"I'll take one of those tankards," he said, indicating my schooner.

Soo was already pulling.

I slapped a stack of bills on the bar.

Dr. Jingler mounted a stool and looked around. "Saw Bad Brains here in '82." He had a gulp from his schooner. "Hasn't changed much."

"I almost fainted when I saw you on the news," I said. "I thought you were going to be a cosmologist."

"I'm a cosmologist at heart, Willie," he said.

"You can call me Eddie," I said. "I think we're safe here among the freaks." I looked over at a glowering Soo. "Present company excluded." I returned my attention to Jingler. "Tell me why meteorology."

"Well, the job was open and weather has always appealed to me. It's the sort of conversation that everyone enjoys having, and much like psychiatry you can't go wrong with a bad prediction. And like psychiatry you have these tremendously vague concepts such as El Niño that explain just about everything. Of course you do get the occasional angry letter from airline pilots and so forth, you know: Granny on *The Beverly Hillbillies* can predict the weather better than you." He had a chuckle and a gulp of beer. "Oh well, you can't please them all."

"Sounds like fun."

"It's a great gig. I belong on TV." He looked me over. "You look good, a little thin. You off the meds?"

"Only taking this," I said, proudly holding up my Asthma Attack.

Soo had primed the jukebox and the air was filled with the steady treacle of Jack Jones and Doris Day. An old kyphotic man entered, hat squashed in his hands, squinting into the darkness and glancing anxiously at a statue of Ahab wielding a harpoon to his left, then down the way at the Jackie Kennedy twins. He smiled when he saw Soo.

Dr. Jingler loosened his tie. "So, tell me what you've been doing with yourself since you jumped into the Napa River?"

"Well, I'm dealing records for a friend of mine. Not a bad living. Playing the horses here and there. And I've got a place up the hill in a little *barrio* my father built back in the fifties."

"*Isla Escondida?*"

"That's it."

"Been there many times," he said. "But not since the poinsettia days. What's on your mind anyway? Your message said urgent."

"Well I'm glad you asked." I finished my beer and gestured Soo for one more.

"Tell me what it is."

"You've heard about the missing Tijuana prostitutes?"

"I've seen the stories."

"For a long time I thought I knew who the killer was. I thought it was my horseracing buddy, Shelly," and here I outlined his terrible childhood, hypochondriasis, necro fantasies, claim of multiple personalities, lack of official identity, the scorch marks on his truck, his deep and unannounced excursions into Tijuana, the scrapbook, the cage in his garage, and his fond assertion that the serial killer is the last anyone ever suspects in the neighborhood.

"Most recreational killers are not recreational gamblers," he observed. "You can only have so much fun."

"Well, they're all different, aren't they?" I said. "I mean you can profile them, but one is an idiot, another like Bundy has an abnormally high IQ, some like Edmund Kemper are funny, some have normal upbringings, hold down regular jobs, are churchgoers, some are married and have children."

"Are you going somewhere with this, Eddie?"

"It's just that, well, I've been going down to Tijuana on a regular basis myself, to visit the brothels, you know, because of my trouble with women and all that stuff you already know about."

He only stared at me, his tankard suspended. "What are you saying?"

"It's just funny that I don't remember much afterward and I always go to church."

"Are you saying you think you might be involved in some way with these missing prostitutes?"

"Well, um, possibly, yes."

"Do you have any specific recollections?"

"I remember names, places."

"Do you have any proof of malice?"

"None," I replied.

"And do you feel imperiled or in any way at risk?"

"Always. But here's the part that bothers me the most. When I decided to drive down to the incinerator at *La Zona Basura* to have a look at it, I had no problem finding it."

"It's a rather obvious structure, billowing smoke and hundreds of feet tall, yes?"

"But I knew right where it was, as if I'd been there before."

"Hmmm."

"And Shelly seems to think I'm the killer because of course I'm the one who was court-mandated to a psychiatric hospital and tagged a sexual predator."

He knuckled his forehead for a time and said, "It seems unlikely that you'd off prostitutes and throw them into a furnace without any recollection of it. I fear that you're falling back into old patterns of figment and fancy."

"Let me buy you another one," I said.

The schooners came. He did not touch his, only kneaded his forehead. "But if you have any real doubts," he said after a good minute of head rubbing. "Test it empirically. Just go down to Tijuana as you usually do and try to find some of these young ladies you've been with. If you can locate enough of them, that should put the matter to rest."

"You're a genius, Dr. Jingler," I said.

"One day I hope to find my true calling," he said.

34.   Back to the Island

I DROVE TO TIJUANA THE NEXT DAY AND PEEKED IN AT A FEW OF THE old hangouts, but I was unable to track down any of my previous *amantes*. Of course, Tijuana is a heaving metropolis, fluid with ever-flowing international humanity, and so after getting a hotel room at the Santa Cruz (which turned out to be gay!) I decided I had no choice but to apply Jingler's test directly. After a late leisurely breakfast I cruised about until I found a cluster of floozies in short skirts out in front of the Miramar Hotel. I parked, got out, engaged a few in light conversation. I found the one who liked me the least and learned that her name was Juanita. She wore black hose, was pale as French bread, and her head was shaped like an oriental vase. I asked, as usual, if she'd like to take a drive to the beach or a restaurant. She said restaurant (*bistek*), quoted her price, and I gave her double up front.

After we had dinner and a drink I considered Jingler's remarks about old habits and changed my mind about having a meaningless liaison with a woman who hated me, thanked her kindly, and dropped her off somewhat puzzled back in front of the Miramar. Feeling better than I had in years, I found a *puesto* that sold Kentucky Fried Buches, or chicken neck tacos served with grilled radish greens and *pico de gallo*, then shopped for records and found a promo seven-inch copy of "Timothy" by the Buoys on Scepter, 1971, with sleeve, the song about three guys trapped in a mine with no food to eat so two of them cannibalize the third, Timothy, a miner with good taste apparently.

I stayed again in Tijuana that night, moving to a hotel not far from the Estadia Caliente, and the following morning I ran into Xena, an eighteen-year-old streetwalker (named after the Warrior Princess on television) I'd known a time or two before. Xena had lustrous plump orange lips and short hair that curled behind her prominent ears. She was thick legged with a big rump and wore white preposterously tall high-heeled shoes. I was so happy to see her I gave her twenty dollars, kissed both of her big ears, and wished her *Feliz Navidad*, even if it was September. She was nonplussed.

Later that day in the *Zona Rio* I found Tamarinda, a tall gaunt woman who specialized in spanking and school uniforms, which normally excited me, but now I was only terribly glad to see her. We went up to her *cuartito* and I just sat with her on the bed. She seemed to be content with this. I read a newspaper for half an hour, the scent of the mattress like Arabian camels and the smoke from train-station cigars. She did not remember me and asked if I was rich. I said no, *(¿de donde?) fuera bueno*, so she decided, as she had the time before, that I must be a student. We talked about the narcos coming in and buying up all the brothels. She said her family back in Michoacán thought she was working here in a *maquiladora*, but she could make three times more in one trick than a whole day of labor in a *maquiladora*. I gave her enough money for twelve days in a *maquiladora* and vigorously shook her hand. Tamarinda was one of the tallest Mexican women I have ever known.

I spent a third day in Tijuana holding on to the good feeling, a pretty nice hotel room (sixteen bucks a night!), and my newfound appreciation for the working class. I fiddled around in the patio shade of a Foreign Book with a couple of peach margaritas and played a card from Churchill Downs without any luck, the way it always was when I played on TV. There was none of the usual excitement and I quit after the fifth race, bought two bottles of Presidente brandy, and headed back to the border.

The sun was going down as I drove up the road to the Island. Halfway up the hill I could see several police cars, two green Border Patrol units, and a horde of uniformed officers swarming the grounds. Beatriz, in her bathrobe, was speaking to them animatedly. Sweets was barking and snarling furiously. Beatriz had him by the collar. I hoped they would not shoot him. I turned my truck around reluctantly and drove as calmly as possible out of there and back down the interstate to Shelly's house.

Shelly was out, no truck in the driveway. I looked for a note and called out his name. Figment and fancy, I told myself as I toured the rooms enduring the usual oppression of anxiety and gloom.

Finally, I called Beatriz. She said my father had been heavily fined for hiring illegal help. The police and *migración* were there "cleaning it up." One tenant had been arrested, another evicted. My father was a *terror* and was talking about selling the land. No matter what happened it was clear that my days were done there, and Beatriz was worried that she would have to move, too. I asked her where she would go and she said likely with her daughter in Temple City. I asked her how Carlito was. She said he seemed depressed and that I should take him if I wanted. I asked her if the police were still there. She said they weren't but thought they would return. I told her I would come pick him up in half an hour, damn the torpedoes. I will take good care of him, I said. I know you will, she said.

35. The Giant Clam Eats Children

SOMEONE IS KNOCKING ON MY WINDOW, THREE A.M. THE CORRI-dors are long with darkly stained wooden floors and silver lines on both sides of the name Decca. The woman in the beehive hairdo is standing a few feet back from the door, the orange tree behind her twinkling, the exhaust spilling like yellow pollen over the sides of the freeway. Like a banshee, she moans his name, "Donny, Donny," and I know she will take him whether or not I open that door.

Before it's too late I must tell Renee that Donny is alive. Obviously, they can't date, or make weak disfigured love, or have children, or plan a stock portfolio, but certain closing words can be pronounced, haunts can be dispelled, horrors and blames laid to rest. I want to tell her also that it was not Shelly's fault. No one pushed Donny or goaded him in. The giant Clam eats children and Donny willingly dove that day into its hungry mouth.

I go into Coco's but Renee is gone. "Quit," Ruby says, "without notice." I drive by her apartment but it looks like she has moved. All the plants on her patio are gone. The car is not there. A rare storm approaches from the east. The sky is green. Renee is walking down the street in tears. I pull up alongside her, roll down the window.

The freeways are empty. The storm behind us grows darker. I cannot remember the city ever being this quiet.

Sweets and I drive west under chowdering clouds. Leaves clack all around us like ghosts on bicycles.

Renee is thinner and younger than I recall in her nightgown, so petulant, so classically spectral.

As you get older chances come along less frequently. The arrow that fate shot long ago has found its mark. You sprawl in regret, feathers in your back, the taste of earth in your mouth. Off to the left is the glitter of a hotel that looks like a chandelier.

I glance over at her legs. She shivers in her evening gown. She is barefoot. There is a Belmonts song on the radio, "Tell Me Why," Surprise Records, 1961. She turns her face to me and says, "I know that Donny is alive."

"Yes, I've been meaning to tell you. He sends his love."

She hugs herself in ecstasy, and I wonder if anyone will ever love me like this.

A gaunt figure in a tattered baggy suit with a suitcase waves at me from the side of the road.

"We're going to fix him up," she says.

"He can't be fixed," I say. "His skull was broken into fifteen pieces."

"Oh no," she says, in the most unconcerned way.

If I did not know I was dreaming, I would tell her about the goddamn sparrows.

Shelly chuckles from the back seat.

My car begins to fill with flowers and the drench of their fragrance.

The three of us wrap Donny in a blanket and throw him over the fence.

There's that shatter of glass and then the melodramatic "Ballad of the Dead Lover," Tragedy Records, 1976.

We watch the bundle engulfed in warm green sea.

36. Love Does Not Experience Time

DAYS PASSED, AND WHILE I WAITED FOR SHELLY TO RETURN, I cleaned his house, resurrected his record business, and wondered where he had gone. The most recent Alabama number he'd given me was out of service. To raise cash I sold the Beatles on Parlophone and continued to comb garage sales and swap meets for valuable records to sell to collectors and dealers on my own.

On my way to a secondhand record store in Kensington on Adams Avenue one day with a copy of T-Bone Walker's "Vida Lee" on Imperial, 1953, I passed a gallery window, slowed, and returned to study a few familiar black-and-white seascape photographs. I went in and asked the gallerist about them. "Can you tell me about the photographer?" I asked.

"Sofia Fouquet?"

"She's still *alive*?" I said.

"Why wouldn't she be? She's thirty-seven."

"Do you have her address?"

"I can't give you that. She once lived in Ferndale, north of San Francisco, now she lives in Ocean Beach."

"Can you call her for me?"

"Of course."

"My name's Eddie Plum."

He dialed the number. I waited. "An Eddie Plum is inquiring about you, Sofia," he said. He put his hand over the phone. "She squealed."

"Can I have it?"

He handed the receiver across and I pressed it to my ear. "Hello."

"Eddie! Is it really you?"

My entire body began to blossom and pop. "My god, Fasstink told me..."

"*Faßtink der schweinpriester!*" she cried. "*Der scheißkauf püpen-pantzen!*"

"Why did you stop writing me?"

"I didn't, the letters just came back. I thought you..."

"Fasstink!"

"*Nüdledich!*"

"Ocean Beach?" I said. "How'd you end up there?"

"I needed a change. Then I heard you broke out. I was hoping to run into you. I'm a longshot player, too."

"Can we meet?"

"Where?"

"Sunset Cliffs?

"No, OB is a dump, a junkie every three feet. Where are you?"

"Inland. San Carlos."

"Apartment?"

"House. Kind of creepy old place."

"Give me directions. I'll see you in an hour."

37. Give Me Stilton, Blue and Gold

I WENT TO THE GROCERY STORE AND BOUGHT A BOTTLE OF GOOD wine and a wedge of the only English cheese they had, a Blue Stilton that you could smell through the wrapper. I straightened the house and had a talk with Sweets.

I've got someone coming over, so I want you to be on your best behavior.

Who?

An old friend. I haven't seen her in years.

A she?

That's right.

Oh, this is bad, he said, staring at me dolefully. *A woman? With your history?*

This one is different.

How?

She was with me at Napa State.

She's a mental patient?

You'll like her. Just give her a chance.

He lunged to chew on his knee and then vigorously kicked his ear with a back paw seven or eight times. *Jesus Christ, I am seriously starting to itch,* he said. *This always happens when I get nervous.*

Listen, I said, *no matter what happens we'll always be together. I promise.* I rubbed him behind the ears, fetched him a pair of tortillas, and went out to wait for Sofia in the driveway.

In no time she rumbled up in a jade green convertible Trans Am, top down, and climbed out. I had forgotten how gracefully she moved. She had changed, of course, it had been many years. She was dressed in slacks and light jacket and gilded sandals, all saffrons and tans and oranges, like a gypsy wrapped in a sunset. A gold scarf was tied around her head. She flashed me one of her quick, secret smiles, removed her sunglasses and walked slowly toward me.

"You look taller," I said, at a loss for words.

"My God, what happened to your face?"

"T-12 troglodyte named Kenny Monique."

I thought she might cry as she embraced me. "He chewed you up pretty good."

"Don't worry," I said, holding her awkwardly. "It's given me the chance to work on my inner beauty."

She pushed me away. "What are you doing in the suburbs?"

"This is Shelly's house. An old racetrack friend."

"Where is he?"

"Disappeared. He does that a lot. Come inside," I said. "I'll show you his museum of suffering."

I pushed open the door. Sweets was sulking in one of the chairs.

"This is Sweets," I introduced. "Formerly Carlito of *Isla Escondida*. He is not a Mexican dog, however."

She patted his head. "Is he yours?"

"He is now."

"He's a handsome boy."

Sweets bumped his tail around and surrendered a flattered, nervous yawn.

I took her through the rooms of Shelly's house, showed her the framed conquistadors in the master bedroom, Donny Ray's shrine, the photographs of Renee, the record room with "Rocket 88," a bottle of Librium thirty-five years expired.

"I know this place," she said. "I grew up in one. Don't tell me, dad fought the commies and never once missed *Lawrence Welk*."

"Something like that," I said.

Back in the living room she paused to run her finger through the dust on my Olympia, then leafed through a few pages of the book I had abandoned. "Shelly's?"

"Mine."

She set her hands on her hips. "So you finally tackled the great American loony bin novel."

"Yeah, I just got to the part where you drove up in your Trans Am."

"I hope it has a happy ending. It is fiction, after all."

"It is." I moved to the kitchen, opened the wine, and poured two glasses.

She took a corner on the crumbling old couch, sipped at the wine. "Is that a television or did someone forget to clean the aquarium?"

"It's a real TV," I said, "the centerpiece of Shelly's museum."

The phone rang. Shelly, I thought, angry about us making fun of his house. We both stared at it until it stopped.

"Every day I think about Napa," she said, removing her scarf and shaking her hair free. "You'll laugh, but it was the most fun I ever had in my life. The singing, the smuggling, *das verböten bedzpringens und humpinderscheetz.* Remember the time you taped the fan of peacock tail feathers to your ass and paraded the grounds?"

"With my dumb haircut and big nose, I even looked like a peacock." I imitated the *hey-yelp* call of the bird.

"What memories!" she cried.

"I've got some English cheese!" I cried.

"No."

"Yes."

"That would be lovely."

I cut a few pieces and set the plate and the knife on the coffee table.

She nibbled, wrinkling her nose. "Scrummy."

"Tastes like socks," I said.

"You never liked food."

"I just forget to eat."

"You look thin."

"I've never seen you in actual *clothes.*"

"What does *that* mean?"

"I wonder if I am dreaming."

"San Diego is too sunny," she announced, popping another cube into her mouth and dusting off her hands. "Don't you think?"

I set my Stilton aside. It was more the stuff you'd put on some-

one's engine manifold for a prank. "It's a beautiful city, everyone tells me."
My head fell over and I feigned sleep.

"So, what do you think happened to your buddy, Shelly?"

"The world keeps changing. He's not equipped for it."

"Is he alone?"

"Always."

"People aren't meant to be alone."

"Are you alone?"

"For the last two years. After I left Murph I moved here. I knew
you were from San Diego. I don't want to talk about Murph."

"I don't want to talk about Murph either." I finished my wine.

Sweets had fallen asleep, head under paw, and was snoring.

"What is this *Isla Escondida* you mentioned?"

I told her about the island and why I would not be able to return.

"We could have our own island," she said.

"Where would that be?"

"Ferndale is nice. It has ocean and redwoods and rain, and there
is not too much sun."

"Is that an invitation?"

"I'm not going to lose you again."

I went into the kitchen and poured two more glasses of wine.

38.   Run Through the Jungler

SIX MONTHS AFTER I LEARNED THAT A CABDRIVER NAMED ROBER-
to Adolfo Malandrin had been stalking and killing prostitutes and throwing their bodies into the great incinerator at *La Zona Basura*, I was pulled
over by a Humboldt County Sheriff who claimed I fit the description of a
psychiatric hospital escapee named Edward Ellington Plum. Driving with
an expired license that was not mine and unable to prove my identity, I was
arrested and taken to jail. Three weeks later came the hearing and I was
remanded to the custody of the state mental health system, this time Atascadero, a maximum-security, all-male forensic hospital in San Luis Obispo
with vomit-yellow halls and pea-soup-colored cells (who chooses the color
schemes for these places?), about two hundred miles south of Napa State,
that specialized in sexual offenders.

Atascadero made Napa look like a Fred Astaire movie. It was
half again as big with many more patient and staff assaults on record and
numerous illustrious deviants such as "The Co-Ed Killer" Edward Kemper, Manson Family member Tex Watson, and Arthur Leigh Allen (likely
Shelly's beloved Zodiac Killer) having signed the registry. ASH was much
more like a prison with tighter security, stricter dress codes, no women
inmates, and no issued ground passes. This was the place you were sent
when you'd been a bad boy at one of the other psychiatric hospitals, where
the recalcitrant, recidivist, and irremediable cases landed, half of them
habitual violent MDSOs (Mentally Disordered Sex Offenders). Once again
I was immediately assigned with MDSOs on Unit 28. I'm certain I was sent
there to be taught a lesson, though this time with stronger resolve I kept
my mouth shut and did what I was told.

Atascadero was an easier place by far to get your head stomped in, but it had its good points too: a big sunny yard and baseball field, large canteen, full-sized movie theater, double the magazine subscriptions in the library, good computer access, and better weather and food than Mudville. Unlike the convoluted corridor networks of ancient madhouses like Napa, there were fewer nooks and crannies, spaces under stairwells, back wards, and recessed doorways where inmates might hide to jump out at you, and so by using the mirrors on each corner you could significantly reduce your odds of getting shanked or crowned by a chair.

I made several key allies here, including a social worker genuinely interested in my welfare who said that if I kept my nose clean the word was I'd be sent back to NSH and maybe even released a year or two down the way. Rumors of Atascadero's infamous sex lab, clandestine psychosurgical unit, and clinical drug-testing programs (in which patients were basically guinea pigs for the pharmaceutical companies) gave me extra incentive to stay on my best behavior. I participated in ward government, manned the diabetic snack wagon, joined the yoga club, and took a pottery class since they did not offer basket weaving. That is just a joke for you, Shelly, wherever you are.

The Atascadero State Hospital Thanksgiving Feast was the first time since I'd been recommitted that I got to see Sofia and my young son, Clive, who had been born with gray eyes that were now green. Sofia was despondent and barely spoke. ("It smells like pine-masked-shit in here," she said at one point, "which I guess is better than that pine-masked-death smell at Napa.") My son, who looked like his mother, shyly and cheerfully had no inkling that he was surrounded by notorious child molesters, several of whom glanced down at him with sly approval.

Jingler, now Jungler, a fundraiser for the Don Quixote Society, came as well, our first reunion since he was a weatherman and we met at Moby Dick's. He was bald with a coarse white mustache, his stomach was more pronounced than his chest, and the wrinkles were deep around his eyes. Since I had been placed in the California Department of Mental Health System on a conservatorship, adjudged on a string of misdemeanors as somehow being "gravely disabled," and I was in no way and had proven extensively to the contrary that I was not "gravely disabled," nor a threat to myself or society, Jungler, familiar with the convoluted parlance of both law and psychiatric institutions, and having dusted off his old counterfeit law degree from the University of Cincinnati (he was Horace Jengler, Attorney at Law, in this incarnation), planned to represent me at my next release hearing in six months and was confident he would get me out.

I was hopeful of this since the Haldol was killing me. The staff was convinced I was an escape risk and did their best to overmedicate me. I had also been assigned a "sitter," someone who watched over me every hour, even staring in at me from a chair outside my room as I slept. Along with the Haldol I was being given Ativan, which like all of the pestilent, nerve-shattering benzodiazepine family, is demonically addictive, opening doors to indescribable horrors and anxieties, another way to get lost forever in the labyrinths of the mental health system.

We ate the turkey, mashed potatoes, dressing, and pumpkin pie—all very good, by the way. I'd like to thank the staff for that, for though these facilities deserve their reputations for savagery, debauchery, corruption, and abuse, you'll also find kindness and even acts of heroism and altruism here. Clive very much liked the pie, especially the whipped cream, and had two slices. Though he called me Daddy, I don't believe he remembered me.

Sofia was going to try to keep the two thoroughbred yearlings I had bought to train, and Clive would soon be enrolled in Montessori. Her parents were helping out financially. My father, who'd sold the Island and all its hothouses and groves of old-growth oak, had also sent a generous check, though he was too disgusted with me to venture through the sally port and the metal detectors to actually visit me. Good behavior and a positive attitude were paramount for my release, so I resisted the temptation to believe he and I would be permanently estranged.

The dinner was over too quickly. As tables were being cleared and stacked and metal chairs were being folded, I kissed my son and wife and promised to send her my almost finished novel soon. She thought *Whirlaway* a good title and hoped that I'd treated her character favorably.

I told her I'd designated her Queen of the Peacocks and Chief Refuter of Salvador Dalí.

"What an asshole that Dalí," she said.

"And tell Sweets I'm sorry for breaking my promise."

She pressed her fingers to her temples, closed her eyes, and said somberly: "I will communicate it to him. But don't you worry about Torti-lla Boy. He is very enamored of your son."

Watching her leaving me once again through the gates to free-dom and wondering if I would ever see her again, I felt suddenly desolate.

She seemed to understand and turned to touch me lightly. "It won't be long this time, Eddie," she said. "I know it in my heart."

My nose began to run, my eyes to burn, and I had to turn away, wishing I was not so thick and confounded by drugs.

Before Jungler left, he gave me a stack of postcards. They were years old, all of them from Shelly who had sent them to cabin number 7 at the Island. I read them in my room as best as I could in the order in which they'd been sent. The last one, postmarked a year before, read:

> Dear Eddie: Donny died today, melanoma. He was forty-two. He went so fast. Unbelievable that my whole family would be gone within the year. Looks like I'll be staying here a lot longer than planned, funeral arrangements, these fly by night policies, one I'm collecting on I told you about that paid three million if Donny died of melanoma before age forty-five, which he went and did. More money than I know what to do with or even care to have, though I expect I'll probably die of cancer here in the next year myself. Until then, Bay Minette is home. I suppose this is my roots, and I've got all my family here, and they've finally stopped haunting me.
>
> Take care. Shelly

Acknowledgments

IT WAS THE READERS IN THE END WHO MADE THE DIFFERENCE IN this book: Marion Winik, who put the ending back on the rails; Steve Taylor, who helped me with my Scottish; Ralph McCarthy, who said whatever you do don't give up on this and recommended I expound on the telepathic dog; Dave Jannetta, who lent me his cinematic eye and told me to get rid of all the instruments of torture; Dave Reutter, who shared with me his expertise on horseracing and the American Loner; my wife, Cristina, who checked all my Spanish; my son, Tom, who listened patiently and often wondrously and reminded me wherever possible to be kind; Scott Parker, who furiously waved those flags as I came in for the landing; Professor Ken Millard, the first of the Great Intellectuals to propose that my work might have scholarly merit; and my publisher and editor, Rhonda Hughes, who doubled the value of this novel with scores of fresh ideas and suggestions on clarity and readability.